A Handful

of

Hope

By Elizabeth Maddrey

Scripture quoted by permission. Quotations designated (NIV) are from THE HOLY BIBLE: NEW INTERNATIONAL VERSION®. NIV®. Copyright © 1973, 1978, 1984 by Biblica. All rights reserved worldwide.

Cover design by Elizabeth Maddrey.
Cover art photos ©iStockphoto.com/Knogami, ©us.fotolia.com/AntonioDiaz, ©us.fotolia.com/leungchopan used by permission.

Published in the United States of America by Elizabeth Maddrey
www.ElizabethMaddrey.com

Publisher's Note: This novel is a work of fiction. Names, characters, places, and incidents are either products of the author's imagination or used fictitiously. All characters are fictional, and any similarity to people living or dead is purely coincidental.

For everyone who has suffered with depression.
Hang in there.
There is hope.

Jen Andrews turned her back to the mirror and craned her neck around. Unfortunately, the back of her dress hadn't miraculously decided to fit. It still made her butt look big. She sighed. Why weren't bridesmaid dresses designed to be flattering? Sure, the bride needed to be the star of the show, but couldn't the attendants at least feel good about themselves? At least the shoes were pretty. She was totally going to wear them again, even if the dress was a waste of a hundred and fifty bucks.

"You look amazing." Sara shut the door to their shared hotel room. She circled her finger in the air.

Jen groaned but circled. "This is not what amazing looks like. Did Rebecca actually think cranberry red was going to look good on us?"

"I think she just got caught up in the whole Christmas Eve wedding thing. Red, green, holly in the bouquets."

"Holly? Really?"

Sara nodded. "So watch your fingers, 'cause I pricked myself about twelve times trying to get them out of their box. I don't understand why the florist didn't trim the pointy bits, but they didn't."

Great. "At least the blood won't show on these dresses."

Sara laughed. Sara slid the closet door open and pulled her dress out. "They're not that bad. And like I said, you're stunning. Have you met your groomsman yet?"

"Not yet. I was surprised when Rebecca said she'd asked Amy and Paige to be in the wedding party, too. I guess it makes sense, sort of, but was there really a problem with you and me walking down the aisle with Jackson and Zach? It's like five minutes, total. Who has—or wants—five attendants?"

"Who knows? I think I caught a glimpse of the two guys. They looked a little familiar. Maybe they were at the party where Ben and Rebecca got engaged?"

Jen shrugged. "Like I said, five minutes max, right? It's not as if we have to become friends. How come you look so much better in this dress than I do?"

"Please." Sara smoothed her hands down her hips. "I thought the A-line was supposed to be flattering, all it does is highlight the fact that I haven't been making time for the gym like I used to. It looks the same as it did on the mannequin on you."

Jen turned sideways and studied her reflection. Maybe Sara was right. She'd never been the best judge of her appearance. Wasn't everyone their own harshest critic? Regardless, she'd managed to drop seven of the fifteen pounds she was working to get rid of. It was a start, at least. "The shoes are killer though."

"Killer's the right word. I don't know why I let you talk me into agreeing to these. I wear sneakers to work. The last time I wore heels was probably my senior prom. And even those weren't three inches high."

"Nothing to it. Just glide."

Sara shook her head. "Right. Or, you know, pray that you don't fall on your face. At least the aisle is very, very short."

"Do Rebecca's parents know this wedding is happening? I know they were planning on it being a surprise, but something like this is bound to slip out, isn't it?" Jen frowned and turned away from the mirror. Why was she obsessing about it anyway? She was here for her friend. Period. If it meant wearing an ugly dress, then so be it.

"As far as I know they're still in the dark. Her mom was just excited to have been able to spend the day at Montepelier and then eat somewhere fancy enough that Rebecca suggested dressing for dinner."

Jen snickered. "That's one way to make sure her mom doesn't end up getting angry about being under-dressed in photos."

"Our gal's a cagey one, that's for sure. And now, we'd probably better high tail it down to the restaurant so we can get the show on the road."

Jen laughed and scooped a small, silk clutch off the bed. "After you."

Sara pulled open the door to their room and Jen followed her into the narrow hallway of the 1700s plantation manor-turned-B&B. The dark espresso stain on the wood floors was polished to within an inch of its life and Jen's heels slipped to the side with each step. She shortened her stride. No point wiping out and giving Sara a reason to laugh and say "I told you so." They went down the narrow, back stairs, avoiding the main lobby where Rebecca and Ben were planning to meet up with their parents. Everyone had agreed that girls showing up in matching dresses would be more of a giveaway than was warranted. Of course, Rebecca's parents were going to have to find out at some point. Wasn't sooner better than later? Jen shrugged. Not her problem.

"Hey guys. You're looking great." Jen waved to Ben's roommates, Jackson and Zach, who huddled at the end of the hall with their fiancées.

Paige grinned. "You, too. Both of you. But Jen...I think you're the only one of the four of us who can really pull off this dress."

Sara's elbow dug into her ribs. "Told you. She thinks she looks fat."

Amy's eyebrows shot up. "Seriously? Do you not have a mirror in your room?"

Jen hunched her shoulders, heat burning across her cheeks. Why couldn't Sara keep her big mouth shut? Time to hedge. "Maybe it's just that the color draws so much attention."

Sara scoffed. "You do usually wear clothes that blend into the background. Anyone seen the other groomsmen? I thought I saw them somewhere, but I'd really like to at least say hi before we're supposed to take their arm."

Paige frowned. "David just ran back to his car for something. He's not staying over, needs to be home for a big family celebration tomorrow, early. I'm not sure where Luc went."

"Luc? Have we even met him before?" Jen sighed. At least David was semi-familiar. She'd heard his name and had probably chatted with him at the picnic in October. She could do this. It was an evening of pretending to be a cheerful person. She did it all the time. Why was it such a struggle tonight?

"I'm right here. And no, I don't believe we've met." Luc extended his hand, a dimple appearing in one cheek. "Luc Duval."

The man was the spitting image of a young version of a famous African American actor. Jen blinked but the comparison remained. She hastily wiped her hand on her dress before taking his. "Hi. I'm Jen. This is Sara."

He tilted his head and shifted his gaze to Sara. His eyes brightened when he saw her and he took her hand, bringing her fingers to his lips. "It's a pleasure to meet you. I understand I'm to be your escort."

That figured. Though David wasn't bad looking, if she remembered correctly. But of course Sara got the movie star look-alike with an exotic accent.

"How fun. You have to tell me about your accent. I'll never be able to place it." Sara's eyelashes fluttered and Jen nearly choked. Laying it on a bit thick. Luc, of course, seemed oblivious.

"Have you never been to Martinique? It's an island paradise and it will always be home." Luc drew Sara's arm through his and pulled her along the hall, still talking.

Jen raised her eyebrows at Paige. "So. I guess we should head to the dining room?"

"Should we wait for Davi—ah, here he comes." Paige took Jackson's hand.

"Sorry, sorry. I left my cell in the car and it isn't that I'm planning on taking calls, but my mom worries and will probably text at some point. If I don't answer, she'll call in the cavalry." He stopped and flashed a bright smile. "Jen, right? David Pak. Good to see you again."

She chuckled. His chatter was warm, friendly, and calmed the conga line that had just started up in her stomach. It didn't hurt that her shoes made her about an inch taller than him. They'd be basically eye-level on a normal shoe day. "Good to see you, too."

"Ready?" He offered her his elbow.

"Sure." She took his arm and walked down the hall to the main doors of the restaurant. Standing just outside the large room, she scanned the space. Rebecca and Ben were seated at a large, round table near the fireplace with both of their parents. What she could see of Rebecca's dress was gorgeous. The style was similar to theirs, but the ivory color and beading on the bodice clearly labeled it a wedding dress. Had her mom really not figured it out yet?

The hostess lifted a finger. "I'll go change the music. They know the cue."

Jen nodded and stepped back, lest any of the parents look up. "It goes Sara and Luc, me and David, Paige and Jackson, then Zach and Amy, right?"

Everyone nodded and shuffled into roughly the right order. It didn't matter, really. But that's what Rebecca had said, so she wanted to at least try and do it right. The music changed from the quiet jazz that had been playing to a string quartet and Pachelbel's Canon in D. Rebecca and Ben looked at each other, smiled, and pushed back from the table, moving to stand in front of the fireplace.

Sara and Luc started through the restaurant doors. Jen and David followed after they'd gone a few steps. Jen grinned as she saw Rebecca's parents exchange a startled look before comprehension slowly dawned. Jen let go of David's arm and moved to stand beside and slightly behind Rebecca with the rest of the bridesmaids.

"Mom, Dad, Mr. and Mrs. Taylor." Rebecca paused and looked at Ben.

Ben took her hand in his. "Wedding planning was getting too complicated. So we decided to elope. But we also wanted you to be with us to celebrate and, more importantly, to witness our vows. Because our promises to God and each other mean more to us than any fancy party ever could."

Rebecca reached out a hand to her parents. "We had a judge sign the marriage license yesterday when we picked it up—that's why our errand took a little longer than we'd planned. But we were hoping, Dad, that you'd say a few words."

Roland MacDonald scooted away from the table, pressing a kiss to his wife's head as he stood. "I'd be honored. It happens that I've been paging through wedding services lately, hoping you'd ask me to do your ceremony. This...is perfect for the two of you. I'm grateful that you'd include us."

Jen blinked away tears. It was good to see Rebecca and her dad working their way back to a less strained relationship. The fact that neither he, nor her mom, were upset was a good sign. She pulled her attention back to Rebecca's dad, who had started speaking.

"That was a nice wedding. Short, sweet, to the point." David shook his napkin and laid it in his lap. "And I should be able to have dinner and still be home soon enough to keep my mom from worrying that I'll miss Christmas morning."

Jen frowned. It had been a nice wedding, but putting it that way seemed...odd. "Not into romance, I take it?"

"Oh. No, I didn't mean it that way. I was happy to play whatever minor part I had getting these two together. I'm still not completely sure what I did, to be honest. Mostly put Ben in touch with a former colleague, Colin. He's the one who did all the work.

I've just been in a lot of weddings lately, with a couple more on the horizon, and..." David shrugged.

Maybe she could see that. She hadn't been in—or to—many weddings lately. But that was about to change now that both of Ben's roommates had set dates. Since Ben and Rebecca got together, Jen and Sara had expanded their circle of friendship to include Paige and Amy. Now both women were including them in wedding plans as well, thankfully not as bridesmaids, but still involved. This was a good thing. Mostly.

"I guess that makes sense. I know we spoke, briefly, at the picnic in October, but that was a while ago. Remind me what you do?" Jen reached for her water glass as the server finished filling it.

"I'm a project manager for a large software company based in Tyson's Corner. We do a lot of Department of Defense contracts, but have commercial solutions as well, though I tend to be in the government space. I was a political science major for a while in college, so I end up doing any of the hobnobbing no one else wants to do."

She nodded. That made sense. Hadn't Rebecca said David was really Jackson's friend? "You like it?"

"Most of the time. Keeps my fingers on the political pulse. What about you?"

"I'm one of the masses programming away all day in Tyson's."

"Where?"

Jen named her company. David started laughing.

"What's funny?"

He shook his head. "It's a big corporation, I knew that. But I thought I'd at least recognize someone who worked in the same office building. I feel like I'm always in the hall or on the elevators."

"That might explain it, then. I'm a get there, work, go home kind of gal. Sometimes I leave for lunch, but most of the time I'm at my desk on the eighth floor. You're what, up on fourteen?"

"Close. Fifteen. I don't get down under ten often at all, that's a completely different division. Makes me feel a little better at least."

Jen nodded and turned her attention to her plate. Now that the basic chit-chat was over, what was there left to talk about? Sara was better at this. Where had she gone? Jen glanced around and sighed. Sara and Luc had moved to a table for two instead of the big round table for all the wedding party. Of course. Everyone else was talking amongst themselves. So it was up to her to try. "You're heading back to northern Virginia after dinner?"

David took a drink of water, swallowing visibly before nodding. "Yeah. Christmas is a big family day for us. Usually everyone—all five of my siblings, their spouses and kids, my aunts and uncles, cousins—has dinner together and spends the night at my grandparents on Christmas Eve so we're all there in the morning. It's a big deal."

"So will you make it? It's got to be getting late." She'd left her phone in her room. The people who'd call her were all here. But since she didn't wear a watch, and the romantically lit dining room didn't have clocks hanging on the walls, she had no idea what time it was.

David pushed back his cuff and glanced at the gold watch on his wrist. "I have about half an hour before I need to go. My mom said she'd make sure they left the door unlocked and set out my sleeping bag in the basement with the rest of the kids."

"Kids?"

He shrugged. "Since I'm still single, and not interested in having my grandfather and father find me a wife, I'm put with the children."

Jen's mouth dropped open and she snapped it shut. People still did that?

"It's not so bad. And at this point, most of my cousins are still there with me, so it's a room full of the twenty-somethings in the family who are too American, if you ask Grandfather at least, to do what's traditional. And then a few of the children from my married cousins who are old enough not to still sleep with their parents."

"That's...different."

David nodded. "It's just once a year. I mean, we get together all the time, but we only spend the night at Christmas. Even if I was married, we'd likely be sharing a room with another couple or two. Big family, you know?"

"I'm an only. Both of my parents were onlys as well. So family gatherings aren't huge. But I can imagine." Chaos. It sounded like chaos. Her stomach twisted. How did you breathe with that much family around? "You like it."

"Most of the time." He grinned. "What about you? You never got lonely?"

Sure she had. Still did, sometimes. Didn't everyone? "Didn't you? You can be lonely in the middle of a crowd, too."

"All right. I'll give you that."

"Mom and I are close though. Dad, too, for that matter. We're a unit. They never let me feel the lack of siblings. I had them."

"And they're okay with you missing Christmas?"

She nodded. "They usually take a trip to an island for New Year's, so this year they just flipped it. They left for St. Croix yesterday. They'll get home the day before New Year's Eve. We'll hang out and do Christmas then."

"You miss them."

Jen gave a half-hearted shrug. She did, but she hadn't been able to swing the cost of the trip anyway. "Like I said, we're a unit."

His watch started beeping and he looked down before silencing it. "I need to hit the road. But...will you be at work next week?"

"Monday through Thursday. Friday's New Year's Eve."

"Want to grab lunch on Tuesday?"

She studied him. He seemed nice enough, and he was cute, but it wasn't as if she'd taken one look across the room and felt her heart start to sing. On the other hand, it was lunch. And making new friends, especially with her current set all pairing off, was never a bad idea. "Sure."

His face lit up and he reached into his shirt pocket to extract his cell. "Really? Cool. Put your number in and I'll give you a call on Monday to confirm."

She took his phone and opened his text messages. She sent a quick text to herself before handing him back the phone. "Now I have your number, too."

David nodded as he slipped his phone back into his pocket. "Talk to you Monday."

2

David slid behind the wheel and started the engine. He cranked the heat to its highest setting, even though it wouldn't start to blow until the engine was warmer. At least knowing the heat was coming kept his teeth from chattering. He scrolled to his grandparent's address in the car's GPS and set the destination. Once he hit the highway he'd be fine, but the B&B was nestled in the middle of nowhere in central Virginia and his sense of direction wasn't strong enough to get him on the right road. At least not on the first try.

He turned right out of the driveway and punched his mother's number.

"David, you're on the way?"

"Hi, Mom. Yeah, I'm leaving now. It says an hour and a half. That's probably close enough."

"We should still be up. Someone got your Uncle Jin talking about his college days."

David chuckled. Uncle Jin could talk for hours and keep everyone in stitches. You'd never know to look at him, but his father's brother was quite the entertainer. "I'm sorry I'm missing it."

"You've heard all the stories before. You know how he and your father get. How was the wedding?"

"Nice, I guess. They got married. No one seemed upset that it was a surprise elopement. The food was good."

"Hmm. But?"

But it wasn't what he wanted. He wanted to get married in their church, to go forward on a Sunday morning as part of the service with his bride on his arm to say their vows. He couldn't tell his mother that, she'd start looking for someone to throw his way. "I wasn't sure what to expect."

The laughing conversation in the background faded. His mother must have moved into a different room. "David, God will bring the right girl your way. I know it's hard to wait and watch as your friends marry, but try not to worry over it too much. Your father and I are proud of you. We raised you, and your siblings, to be men and women who put God first. And you do. Keep doing that and when the right girl comes along, you'll know."

Jen's smiling face as she watched Rebecca and Ben kiss at the end of the ceremony flashed through his mind. "What if she's not Korean?"

His chest constricted. Had he just said that out loud? David cringed, turning when the navigation system dinged. Signs for the interstate glowed ahead. Maybe his mother hadn't heard him.

"If she's the woman who God truly has for you, then your grandparents will adjust. It might be a hard sell, but you know your father and I will support you." Humor trickled into her voice. "Still, they won't object to God's direction for your life. What's her name?"

David eased the car into the on-ramp. "I don't have anyone in particular in mind. I'm...not sure where that came from."

"Mmmhmm." He waited for her to push. She'd always known when he tried to get something past her. "Drive safely, honey. I'll see you soon."

He ended the call and pressed down on the accelerator. What had he been thinking? He hadn't been thinking, obviously. He'd met Jen twice. Both times for less than two hours. Maybe they'd had a good conversation about nothing tonight, but marriage? Did he want to see her again, get to know her better? Yes. There was a pull there. Did she feel it? She didn't give any indication that she did. But wanting to get to know someone was a far cry from asking her to share the rest of your days.

He'd keep reminding himself of that. And maybe he'd find a way to forget the tingling warmth that had spread through him when she took his arm.

David wiped sweaty palms on his jeans. This was lunch with a friend. Or, sort of a friend. Friend of a friend's friend? He stepped off the elevator when it stopped on her floor. Had he ever even been here? He checked his watch.

Jen stepped through an unmarked door and stopped short. "I'm not late, am I?"

"No, you're early. I'm early." He smiled and gave himself a mental kick. Stop being an idiot. "I can wait if you're not ready."

"It's fine, we can go. Where'd you want to eat?"

David cleared his throat. He'd considered the cafeteria or the place across the street, but the food was average on a good day at both places. And if she was anything like most of the employees, she'd eaten at one or the other so often neither would rank high on the list unless starvation was imminent. Which meant driving somewhere or a long-ish walk. "Do you like Peruvian chicken?"

"If it's good, I love it. I haven't found one in Tyson's that I love though."

"Hmm. Have you been to Peru Chix? It's hidden behind a car dealership down a few blocks." David hooked his thumbs in his pockets. He had backup ideas, but he'd been dreaming about the chicken since Christmas.

Jen shook her head. "I haven't even heard of that one. Let's give it a try."

"Excellent. Come on, I'll drive." He pushed the button for the elevator. Apparently no one needed it after he got off. It dinged and opened the doors immediately. When they were in, he pushed the button for the garage. "Did you have a good Christmas?"

"It was okay. Got to video chat with my parents for a bit and see the beach, even if I couldn't be there with them. Then I spent the rest of the day working on the five thousand piece puzzle they got me."

He coughed. "Five thousand pieces? That's a big puzzle. You finished it?"

Jen laughed. "No. Not even close. But I got about half of the border put together. And I got caught up on most of the shows I stream. How was your family thing?"

She sounded lonely. And a little sad. Probably better not to mention that though. The elevator stopped and he gestured for her to go first, pointing to the car in the closest spot. "This is me. My day was good. I enjoy spending time with my family. And when everyone's there it's this big, crazy explosion of laughter and noise. I wouldn't want to do it every day, but I like it."

"Everyone still lives in the area?" She slid into the car, offering a smile as he pushed the door closed.

He rounded the hood and got in. "Most of us. Some of my dad's siblings have moved to Richmond or Charlottesville. But that's still close enough for them to make the major holidays without too much trouble."

"And your mom's family?"

David started the engine. "They're all in California. We don't see them that often. Mom tries to go out once a year though. Where's your extended family?"

"My mom's parents are divorced. Both remarried, but neither is able to be polite to the other still, and they try to put her in the middle. So we don't see them...at all, really. I think the last time I saw either of her parents I was in middle school. Dad's parents are still married, but they're missionaries in Thailand. It's a lot cheaper to get to the Caribbean than Asia. They haven't been back to the states in five years or so. And when they are back, they're usually busy fundraising, not simply vacationing." Jen shrugged.

What would that be like? He shook his head; the picture just wouldn't form. She seemed fine with it—why wouldn't she be? It was her normal. What would she think of his family? Would they be too much for her? Maybe it was too soon to worry about it, but...Mom was already pressing, unwilling to let go of his slip on the phone. David pulled into a parking spot outside a dilapidated storefront. "Here we are. Don't let the look fool you, the food's great."

David leaned away from his monitor and turned to look out the window. When was the last time he'd enjoyed lunch with someone that much? Jen was funny and real and just...fascinating. But she gave no indication whether or not she felt the same way. Was there any possibility of this becoming more? Was it even realistic to want it?

His parents...would be okay with it. They'd grown up in America and had always encouraged him and his siblings to be Americans. Understand Korean culture, yes, but not hold to it for the sake of history. And even then, Jesus was more important. His family was deeply rooted in Christ, thanks to the missionaries who had visited his grandparent's village and, in the end, helped them flee. But his grandparents would be disappointed. Did it matter? He hated to disappoint anyone. He'd been brought up to respect and honor his elders. But loving Jen wasn't dishonoring them, was it?

Not that he was in love. But he could see it happening down the road.

The phone on his desk rang. Just as well, since he wasn't making any great mental strides.

"David Pak."

"Hey, little brother. Figured you'd be at work today."

He chuckled. "Hi, Ji-Yoon. You're not working?"

"Oh, fine. Yes, I'm at work too. But that's mostly because Min took the kids down to the zoo so I could. There's a big deadline the second week of January and it's giving me anxiety."

"Make any headway?" His sister was a worrier. Probably came from being the oldest of six and, essentially, a second mother to the youngest three.

"Enough that I can start sleeping at night again. Not why I called though. Mom says you met someone?"

David banged his head against the back of the chair. "Maybe. I don't know."

"Hmm. Sounds serious."

He frowned at the laughter in her voice. "I met her for the second time on Christmas Eve—really the first time. We barely said hello the first time we were in the same place. And I don't know if she's even interested."

"Is she stupid?"

"What kind of question is that? She's a programmer, same company, actually, though I hadn't realized that."

Ji's laugh was like tinkling glass. "If she's not stupid, she's interested. When do we get to meet her?"

He cringed. "Can we hold off on that for a while? Like maybe until we've been actually dating for a few months?"

"I suppose that's fair. What about just me?"

"Mom's curious, isn't she?"

"You always were smart. Mom said this girl's not Korean?"

David pinched his nose. "No."

"Cool. You know I don't care, right? I nearly married Jared, if you recall."

Jared. David hadn't thought of him in years. Even though he'd just been a kid when Ji was dating him, their break-up had shaken the family. Not because he was white, but because he'd had the lack of class to cheat on Ji and get caught by Dad. David had never seen his usually soft-spoken, mild-mannered father so close to violence before or since. "Close shave there."

"That it was. But my point is that it doesn't matter. To me, or to Mom and Dad. So you shouldn't worry about that."

He chuckled. "How'd you know?"

"I know you, little brother. Tell you what, maybe after the New Year, you can ask her to lunch and happen to run into me. Then it's not as intimidating as asking her to meet your family—or even just your older sister. And I can get back to Mom and everyone will be happy."

Maybe not everyone. But it was inevitable. If he'd managed to keep his mouth shut...but he hadn't. Which meant this was the least horrific option. "Yeah, okay. I'll let you know. Kiss my niece and nephew for me."

"That I will. They're still enamored with the stop motion movie set you gave them, you hit a home run with that one. It's been 'Uncle David' this and 'Uncle David' that all weekend. Don't forget about lunch though. Got it?"

He smiled. "Got it. Bye, Ji."

3

Jen kicked off her shoes and left them where they fell. Lunch with David had been pleasant. And filling. Which got her out of having to figure out dinner. She could find a snack and call it good.

"But you're hungry, Tribble, aren't you?" She squatted by the crate where her silky terrier quivered with excitement. "Come on, we'll go for a little walk and then get you some food."

Jen clipped the leash to Tribble's collar and slid her feet into the flip-flops she kept by the back door. The ground-level apartment had the added bonus of being just three short steps from a grassy area, which made walking Tribble much less of a chore. The small dog didn't need long walks—or runs—for exercise. She just needed a place to do her business that wasn't the carpet. Jen could toss the ball while she worked on the puzzle and the little dog would get plenty of running.

After they'd made three circuits of the square patch of lawn, Tribble bounced toward the sliding glass door of Jen's apartment. Ready to eat. Jen smiled. Dogs were good reminders of how to keep life basic. All you needed was someone to love you, food, a place to play, and naps. Her smile faded. Her parents loved her, so did God, but wouldn't it be nice to have someone else, someone who didn't have to love her but did anyway, because they wanted to? It wasn't likely to happen. Even if it did, how long would it last? She could put on the happy front at work and with friends, but when she was home, it was nice not to have to force the smile and act like getting out of bed wasn't the hardest thing she'd done that day.

Jen checked to be sure the patio door was locked and the nails, top and bottom, that were supposed to keep would-be robbers from being able to jimmy the door off its track, firmly in place before pushing thoughts of love from her mind and angling into the kitchen.

"Come on, Trib. I think tonight's a night for beef stew. There's just enough nip in the air to justify the treat." She unclipped the leash and hung it back up by the door.

Tribble's ears perked up at the word 'treat' and she whined before yipping and scurrying into the kitchen where she pranced in place for a moment before dropping into a perfect, lady-like sit in front of her bowl. Jen popped the top of the small can of dog food, wrinkling her nose as the wet, not-quite-meaty smell filled the room.

"I don't know how you eat this stuff." She stuck out her tongue and spooned the gloppy mixture out. Tribble quivered, a tiny rope of drool escaping from her mouth as her brown eyes followed the spoon on its course from can to bowl and back again. "Good girl. Eat."

Tribble bolted forward and began devouring her meal as the doorbell buzzed.

Who on Earth? Jen checked the time as she passed by the stove. It wasn't late, but she wasn't expecting anyone. She peeked through the spy hole in the door and sighed. Sara. Turning the locks, Jen tugged open the door. "I wasn't expecting to see you tonight."

Sara grinned and started to pull Jen into a hug, stopping midway with a pained look on her face. "What is that smell?"

Jen sniffed and glanced down at the dog food can still in her hand, the spoon lolling around within. "Sorry, I was just—"

"You're not eating that, are you?" Sara made a gagging face as she pushed the door closed behind her.

"Ha ha. No. It's for Trib, figured it could be a treat night. Did you have dinner yet?" Jen ambled back into the kitchen and rinsed out the can before dropping it into the recycling bin under the sink and washing her hands. Hopefully Sara *had* eaten. But if Jen didn't offer, she'd be setting herself up for another lecture on good nutrition and the importance of small meals spaced throughout the day rather than one big lunch and a whole lot of water. Jen wasn't in the mood to hear it.

Sara angled her head to the side and studied Jen as she came back into the living room. "I did. Did you?"

"Not yet. I had a huge lunch. I'll eat something, I promise. Just later, okay?" She'd at least have a cracker before bed. Then it wasn't a complete lie. Better to change the subject before Sara pursued the topic. "So what brings you by?"

Her friend's face morphed into an angelic grin, the glow nearly blinding. "Luc. Oh, Jen. I think I'm in love."

Jen's eyebrows shot up. "That was fast."

Sara dropped onto Jen's couch, kicked off her shoes, and tucked her feet under her. "Don't be that way. We have a *connection*."

Jen fought the urge to roll her eyes and lowered herself into her comfy chair. It was her favorite garage sale find, ugly as an alley cat under the cheerful hot-pink slip cover, but sitting in it was like floating on a cloud. She propped her feet on the dark purple ottoman she'd made from an old plastic milk crate, some quilt batting, and scraps of fabric her mom had floating around in her craft room. "What kind of connection?"

Sara's hands flew around wildly. "Just...a *soul* connection. He understands me. We can talk for hours at a time—have been, since Thursday. He's so amazing."

"Sara." Jen licked her lips and tried to organize her thoughts. Tribble darted out of the kitchen and jumped up on the couch with a yip, then crawled into Sara's lap. Sara grinned and scratched behind the dog's ears before looking back at Jen with an expectant expression. "Go slow, okay? Wasn't it about this time last month that you were in love with Paul. It was Paul, right? And before him was, oh what was his name?"

"George. His name was George. And I see what you're saying. But this is different."

It was always different. Except it never was. Sara went through men like tissue paper, soaring from high to earth-crashing thuds in days. For a while last year, she'd managed some kind of sanity in her dating life, and then something happened and she was back to her old habits of the Man of the Month. "What's different this time?"

Sara sighed, her face crumpling into a frown. "I knew better than to come here. Why would you understand? When was the last time you had a date, anyway?"

"Lunch."

Her friend straightened, a gleam in her eye. "How did I not know about this? Why didn't you call me? Who? Where? I need details."

Why had she said that? Too late to backpedal now though. Jen huffed out a little sigh. "David. Turns out, we work in the same building."

Sara scoffed. "You and half the population of the area work in that building or the one next door. Your company is..."

"Anyway, at the wedding, we got to talking and he asked if I'd like to do lunch. I said yes." Better to stop the tirade about large international software companies before it could start. Not every company could stay a small, local business. Not everyone wanted to work for that sort of place. You couldn't be anonymous in a tiny office and Jen didn't want the problems that came with that. She liked being a worker bee—go in, do her job, go home. Period, end of story.

"And?" Sara leaned forward, eliciting a grumble from Tribble who hopped off the couch and went to her dog bed, grabbed her favorite squeaky toy, and started gnawing. "Ugh. Why do you get her those things? Don't they drive you insane?"

Jen shrugged. "She likes them and the squeakers break eventually."

"If you say so." Sara glared at the dog before turning her attention back to Jen. "David? He's good looking, got that boy next door thing going on, which I know you like."

"As opposed to the international man of mystery vibe Luc gives off? Yes, I like the boy next door. At least with him, I can figure out where he lives."

"Whatever. We're not talking about Luc right now. Spill."

Jen had been considering calling Sara to talk about lunch and try to work through her thoughts—get a better hand on them. But now...maybe she wasn't ready to share yet. "He's nice. A gentleman—opens doors and everything."

"Oooh. Points for him. Brave, too, since today you're as likely to get your head ripped off as thanked for doing something like that. It all depends on the girl."

Jen chuckled. She'd said something along those lines to him. He said his dimples usually got him out of trouble, even with the sternest objectors. Boyish charm; he had it by the bucketful. "We have a lot in common, though he's moved into management and I'm content to program. There's not a lot to tell. We're just getting to know each other right now, you know?"

Sara nodded.

"What?"

"Just trying to decide if that was a dig."

Jen wrinkled her brow. "How would that be a dig? It's just...what we're doing."

"Luc...you're saying I don't know him."

She hadn't been. Not that it wasn't true, but that hadn't been why she said it. Jen shook her head. "I wasn't—"

"You're not wrong. But he's so exotic and fascinating. That accent and his dark, gorgeous skin." Sara let out a dreamy sigh.

"What does he do for a living?"

Sara blinked, frowning. "Um. I...don't know. I'm sure he told me. Doesn't he work with Ben? Why else would he be at their wedding?"

Okay. Shouldn't that be one of the first things you talk about? In that whole introducing yourself stage of things? "So he's local? Not based in, where was it?"

"Martinique." The dreamy look was back. "I...assume so. He didn't really say."

"Well, what *did* he say?" Jen crossed her arms. Something about this guy was starting to sound weird. She liked Ben. She liked him a lot. And he and Rebecca were a great couple. But if they were in a rush to add attendants, did he choose someone he knew really well, or just a coworker who happened to be available?

"All kinds of things. Look, just because you're doing something one way doesn't mean my way is wrong because it's different. I should go." Sara stood, stuffing her feet back into her discarded shoes. "When Rebecca's back from her honeymoon we should get together for lunch."

Jen nodded, standing. "Don't be mad at me. I'm glad you're happy. I just don't want to see you get hurt."

Sara shook her head. "Luc won't hurt me."

"You look wonderful, Mom. St. Croix agrees with you." Jen let her mother fold her into a tight hug. She'd said she was all right with not having Christmas together but...something had been missing. This made it better. She'd have to start saving now so she could go wherever they settled on next year. Or not be too proud to let them pay for her.

"Thanks, Jennifer. You're looking lovely as well. Though I do wish you'd come with us. I understand wanting to pay your own way, but it would've been our pleasure. In more ways than one. I missed my baby girl."

Jen's dad came in, holding three flutes of sparkling cider. "So did I."

"Well, that makes three of us." Jen chuckled and accepted the drink. "I was just thinking I'd start saving money and vacation days now so wherever you decide to go next year, I can come. Though, presumably, I won't have a last-minute wedding to worry about putting a wrench in the plans."

Her mom crossed to the sofa and patted the seat next to her. "How was the wedding? Did you take any photos?"

Dad sat in a chair facing them. "More to the point, did her parents do okay?"

"It was good. Simple and short. And her parents seemed genuinely pleased. I think they'll still have a reception in Texas at some point, but with the wedding out of the way, they can take their time on scheduling that." Jen patted her pockets and stood. "I think I have a few pictures on my phone, which is apparently in my purse."

"Go get it. Are we working on your puzzle tonight? Or did you want to play a board game instead?"

Jen dug in her purse for her phone and returned to the couch. "I already started the puzzle, so it's at home. Sorry. I needed something to do on Christmas day."

"Oh, sweetie. I'm sorry. We never should have gone." Her mom rubbed Jen's leg. Tribble jumped up into Jen's lap and licked her mom's hand, making the older woman laugh and rub behind her ears. "Sweet thing. Is your mom letting you help with the puzzle, too?"

Jen snickered. "She's trying, but somehow her help isn't quite as useful as you'd imagine. What on earth possessed you to get a five-thousand-piece puzzle? I'll be working on it for the rest of my life. Which means I'll never eat at my dining room table again. Did you realize it's going to be five feet by three feet when it's finished?"

"That big?" Jen's dad shook his head. "I left the purchasing to your mother, so you can't blame me. But...maybe you could build it in segments?"

"Both of you stop being so silly. You'll have it finished in no time, Jen, I know you. Now show me those photos. I want to know all the details."

Jen swiped to the beginning of the photos and angled the phone so her mom could see. "This is the B&B..."

"Lovely." Her mother swiped to the next photo. "Oh, don't you and Sara look lovely. That dress is amazing on you. We'll have to see if we can find another place for you to wear it. A Valentine's Day dinner, maybe?"

"Mom. There's no one to go to a Valentine's Day dinner with." Even as she said the words, she had a flash of David's smiling face, the barest hint of a dimple in his cheek.

"Hm, well, it's not even the new year yet. There's time." Her mom swiped to the next photo and hummed again. "Who's this?"

Jen looked down, heat crawled across her cheeks. She'd been goofing around with David at the dinner table, taking selfies. "That's David Pak, he was the groomsman I was paired with. A friend of Jackson's, actually, but I guess he helped Ben court Rebecca somehow. I'm not clear on the details, to be honest."

Her mom's gaze was piercing.

"What?"

"You're blushing. Tell me more." Jen's mom swiped to the next photo, another of her and David goofing around.

"Yes, do." Her dad crossed the room and sat on the couch, peering down at the phone. "When do we get to meet him?"

Meet him? "Wh—no. It's not like that. We're just, we aren't, we only sat together at the wedding."

Her dad chuckled. "I'm not convinced, but we can hold off. For now. What's he do?"

Jen's tongue darted between her lips. "He's a project manager at my company. Different division—realistically we'd never have even run into each other, despite working in the same building."

Her parents exchanged a look before her mother spoke. "Well. Your father and I met at work."

How had she forgotten that? They told the story at every possible opportunity. They'd been so...proud, maybe...that they didn't meet in college like all their friends. They both had careers first. "It was a wedding, Mom. I doubt—"

"He hasn't called you?" Her dad reached for the phone and changed the photo.

"We had lunch on Tuesday. But that wasn't anything. He was just being nice." Jen reached for her phone. It was time to stop talking about David. He hadn't called, or emailed, texted, anything since. And really, who could blame him? She wasn't anything special. Smart, sure, but incredibly average when you looked at her. David...was on an entirely different plane. "Are we looking at my phone all night, or ringing in the New Year with a board game like we're supposed to?"

4

David stretched his arms over his head and groaned. Everyone on the team was back from their vacations and the quiet, peaceful week between Christmas and New Year's when he'd been able to get work done during business hours was gone. For the past four days, it had been meeting after meeting as people tried to remember what they'd been doing before the holidays. Two of the projects he was managing had deadlines looming at the end of January and both had key players who'd used their time off to find new employment. Not an auspicious start to the year.

"Got a second?" Stephen, the team lead for one of the projects now facing certain doom stood in his doorway.

"Yeah, of course. Come in." Stephen closed the door and crossed to David's desk. David's stomach sank. There was no cheerful reason for Stephen to need privacy. "What's up?"

Stephen rubbed the back of his neck. "There's no good way to say this. I'm leaving at the end of the month. I have my resignation ready to send, but after the bombshells in the meeting this morning, I thought I'd tell you in person beforehand."

David closed his eyes and swallowed before forcing a strained smile. "Where are you going?"

Stephen named a smaller company—one they frequently used as a sub-contractor—and the same place their key programmer was going, if the rumor mill was to be believed. "I've loved my time here. I know I owe a lot of that to you. When you started moving up, you took the rest of us who'd started about the same time with you. But there's so much paperwork and meetings now...I like leading a team, but I want to keep my hand in development, too. There's not really a career path here that would allow that."

David nodded. That was true, if only because of the bureaucracy that came from working in a big company. Personally, programming had never been something he loved. After giving up on political science, he'd majored in business with a computer science minor only to provide more options for getting his foot in the door. Management was where he'd been headed from day one. If he tried, he could understand how that might not be ideal for someone more interested in code. Still. "We have some senior developer positions open in the architect track. I could look into transferring you. That would ease the management requirements and increase your development time. Plus, it would come with a salary bump."

"I...would I stay on this project?" Stephen frowned and clasped his hands together.

"Do you want to?" David held Stephen's gaze. He could make it work either way—he'd certainly rather keep Stephen, but the company overall would be better served if Stephen stayed, even if it meant changing divisions.

"Maybe. I don't know. What about the team lead stuff? Who'd do that?"

David shrugged. "We'd find a replacement for your current position, most likely. Or, in the interim, I'd take it on. You don't have to decide right away, take a week to think about it and let me know."

"Okay. Thanks, David." Stephen stood and held out his hand.

David shook it and smiled. Hopefully Stephen'd decide to stay—and stay on the project. He already had a voicemail from his boss asking what was going on with his projects. Losing another employee was not going to go over well. At all. Plus, Stephen was a solid worker. Even without the scrutiny he'd come under with three employees leaving at the same time, losing Stephen would be a hit to the team's productivity. "Any time. I appreciate you coming to me in person."

When Stephen left, David leaned back and stared at the ceiling. Generally, people didn't take counter offers. Or, if they did, they didn't stay very long afterward. But he'd had to try. He also needed to get his feelers out and see if there was someone who might be interested in transferring to his project. He'd send a quick email to his contact in HR and have him keep an eye out for contracts that were ending. Internal transfers were easier all around than sourcing from the outside.

His stomach growled and he glanced at his watch. After two and he still hadn't had time for lunch. And it was late enough now there was no possibility that Jen wouldn't have eaten. Which meant one more day without a reason to casually swing by. He could text her...and say what? He couldn't guarantee that he'd be free for lunch tomorrow. He could ask her out to dinner over the weekend but that seemed premature somehow. Rushing her wasn't a good idea. What he needed was a party where they could randomly bump into one another. Except that Ben and Rebecca were still on their honeymoon, so even if he could talk Jackson into having one, would he think to invite Jen?

David sighed and ran a hand through his hair. This was like high school. Except worse. Because now, if he did manage to figure out how to ask her out, and she accepted, and they got into a relationship...now his family would insist on getting to know her, too. They'd be nice, they were good people. But he found them overwhelming sometimes, and he was used to them. They'd scare her off in two seconds flat.

So what was he supposed to do?

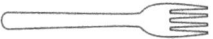

"Hey, man. Glad you could make it." Jackson clapped David on the back and pulled open the door to Season's Bounty.

"Me, too. I appreciate the invite. I hadn't expected you to be free tonight when I called—just thought we could get something on the calendar." David followed behind Jackson as he wound through the tables and pushed open the door into the kitchen.

"Hi, Paige." Jackson poked his head between the expediting shelves before pointing to the four-person banquette stuffed into a corner of the kitchen area.

It was hot. Steamy hot. But the smells mixing in the air set David's stomach in motion. The granola bar he'd eaten at his desk after Stephen left was too little, too long ago. Did they order, like normal? He hadn't seen a menu. David slid into the booth and waited for Jackson. He'd follow his friend's lead on the food.

"Go and sit, Jackson, I'll be out in a minute."

David didn't see her, but that had to be Paige hollering over the clatter of pots and pans. Jackson sat across from David and laid his arm across the seat back. "She'll be here with food when she gets a chance. On the one hand, you never know what you're getting. On the other, I haven't had a loser yet. And she doesn't charge me, though I usually try to pay at the front as I'm leaving. Sometimes they can slide it past her. So how come you don't have a hot date tonight? What happened to...oh, what was her name, Sue?"

Soo Yi. He hadn't thought of her in ages. "We broke up a year ago. My parents were more upset by it than I was. She's engaged to the youth pastor at our church now. They make a good couple. Better than we were."

Jackson winced. "That's not awkward?"

David shrugged. "Maybe a little, but my whole family goes to that church, I'm not going to leave just because it's a little weird."

"No one else since then?"

"Not really. In the aftermath of Soo Yi, I realized I needed to be more careful and only date someone if I was interested in the long haul. Marriage, family, the works. I'm nearly thirty. Dating for fun was fine in college, but now, it's too much work. I'm guessing that makes sense, given that you're engaged now."

Jackson chuckled.

"Hi, honey." Paige scurried to the table, holding a large, rectangular plate laden with bruschetta and two smaller plates. She leaned over and gave Jackson a quick kiss. "Hi, David. It's good to see you. I know I haven't seen you back here, but have you been to the restaurant before?"

David shook his head. "I keep meaning to. I've actually stopped by twice, but the wait was longer than my stomach wanted, so I promised myself I'd try again. Sorry."

Paige waved away his apology. "Please. I'm glad you could come tonight, and hanging out back here is better, anyway. Not that the menu's bad, mind you, but I've been playing with some dishes for spring, you two get to be my guinea pigs."

"Spring menu? It's the first week of January."

She grinned. "I know. And I'm cheating a little, using some of my frozen or preserved vegetables instead of the fresh that I'm hoping will start becoming available late spring. But if they're good, I might put a few of them on for the rest of winter. Other people have to be craving new flavors too, don't they?"

Craving new flavors? Had he ever craved a flavor? It sounded like a girl thing. Or a foodie thing. He was neither, but he nodded. "Sure. This looks good."

"Dig in, man." Jackson took a slice of toast from the tray, maneuvered a large bite into his mouth, and set the rest down on his plate while he chewed. "Mmmm."

David copied Jackson, his eyebrows lifting as the flavors of the tomatoes and peppers hit his tongue. "What's on top? It's amazing."

Paige beamed. "It's a chutney I make. You like it?"

"Oh, yeah. They still taste fresh."

"That's the idea. Glad you like it. Can I get you something to drink? I have an interesting limeade that we're testing out, if you want."

Interesting? That sounded...scary.

Jackson winced. "Define 'interesting.'"

Paige shook her head. "Just try it, okay? I'll send some over. I'd better get back. Things are going smoothly tonight, but you never know when that's going to change. I'll bring another plate before too long though. When's Jen getting here?"

Jen? Jen was coming? David blinked and looked at Jackson. "You invited Jen?"

Jackson shook his head and turned to Paige. "Was I supposed to invite her?"

"Oh. No. I just thought...you looked so cute together at the wedding, David, I thought that might be why you were here." Pink burned across Paige's cheeks. "I'll just go get back to work."

Jackson watched Paige leave before meeting and holding David's gaze. "So. You and Jen?"

David shook his head. "No. Not yet, at least. I'm thinking about seeing where things go. But I don't even know if she'd be interested. We had lunch once after the wedding, before New Year's, but work has been insane and I haven't had a chance to ask her again. But she hasn't reached out, either...maybe that's my cue to leave it be?"

"Are you asking for advice?"

David shrugged. "I guess I am."

"Do you like her?" Jackson pulled another piece of bread from the tray to his plate.

David nodded. "She's the first woman who's interested me in a long while."

"Then make the time."

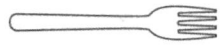

Make the time. David sipped coffee from a white foam cup and looked over the rim at the swirling dance of fellowship and mingling in the foyer of the small, Korean church he'd been attending since he was an infant. Snippets of conversations, all in Korean, floated past, teasing a smile from his lips. What would it sound like to an outsider who spoke no Korean? He closed his eyes, but the conversations continued to be intelligible. He sighed.

"What are you doing?" His sister, Ji, nudged him with her elbow.

Heat crept up the back of his neck. "Wondering what this would sound like if I didn't speak Korean."

Ji nodded. "And?"

David shrugged. "I can't figure out how to *not* understand Korean. So it was a pretty pointless exercise."

She laughed. "You don't have to keep coming to church here. You know that, right? Mom and Dad would understand."

"I know. They've told me that, too." Had made a point of it after they got over him breaking up with Soo Yi. "But this is home. Just as much as Mom and Dad's house is home. I missed it when I was at school and was glad to come back."

"It's not exactly bustling with single people. You're not going to meet your wife here. You know that, right?"

He sighed, his heart sinking. The lack of options had been the largest push for him to date Soo Yi in the first place. Look how well that had turned out. His sister was right. Unless there was a huge influx of young, single women to the church next week, his wife wasn't waiting to be found here. But did he need to change churches to find her? What if they'd already met? "I know."

Ji nodded. "Even if this girl..."

"Jen. Her name is Jen."

Ji flashed a grin. "Even if Jen is the one for you and you no longer have to worry about finding your mate at church, it might be time for you to spread your wings. It's not as if you can't come back."

"I guess. What about Grandpa and Grandma though?"

"What about them? They love you and want you to be happy. Will they be sad if you change churches? Maybe. But it isn't as if you're moving away. Even if you did move across the country, they'd adjust. They always have. Despite being the most American of us,

David, sometimes I worry that you care too much what other people think and not enough about what you want."

He drew his brows together. "I don't—"

"You did so much more 'normal' kid stuff than we did. Did you ever take a lunch to school that was different than your friends'?"

He shook his head. Ji—and his other siblings—always used to complain about leftovers in their lunch sacks. By the time he was going to school, it'd been ham sandwiches and packaged cupcakes or a bag of chips. His parents had even spoken English when his friends were over. Hadn't they done that for the others? He couldn't remember. Maybe he had had a more American childhood than his siblings, that didn't take away the desire to please his parents, to know that they approved of his choices. They'd done so much for him, he wanted to give them the respect they were due.

"It's good that you're respectful and that you value the family. You're a good son and my favorite little brother. But I think it's time—and I think Mom and Dad would agree—that you figured out what God wants for you and worried about that, instead of what you think your family wants. Now come on, they're going to start the service soon."

David tossed his cold, barely-touched coffee into the trash and followed his sister. She slipped her arm through her husband's and herded their kids in front of her. They were their own family. A tiny, cohesive, unit in the larger whole of the Pak clan. Could he find that for himself? *Father God, only You know the plans You have for me. Is Jen...is she part of them? I don't know what to do—have I been avoiding hearing Your voice and listening only to what I thought my family expected? I could use some guidance. Please?*

5

Jen slid into the pew next to Sara and clamped her jaw shut. Luc? She'd brought Luc to church? Not that she shouldn't have brought him. Church was a good date...it was just...there was something off about that guy. And Sara was completely oblivious. She nudged her friend with her elbow.

"What? Oh, hey Jen. You remember Luc?" Sara leaned back as she gestured to the too-good-looking-to-be-true man.

Jen lifted her fingers. "I thought you'd be back in, where was it? Martinique? By now."

"Not when there's someone as lovely as Sara to keep me here." He took Sara's hand and lifted her knuckles to her lips.

Red stained Sara's cheeks and stars shone from her eyes. "Isn't he amazing?"

"I guess. I thought we were doing lunch after the service today?" Jen frowned. Lunch after church was a tradition and she hadn't planned on it stopping just because Rebecca was married.

"Yeah. I just figured Luc..."

Jen shook her head. "Never mind."

"What? He's not..."

"No. Look, you don't bring dates to girls' lunch. Rebecca never did and she actually knew Ben."

Sara bristled. "I do know him. I don't know what your problem is, but you need to get over it."

Jen stood. "I think I'll see what seating in the balcony is like. I've always wondered."

"Don't be an idiot." Sara snatched at her sleeve.

Jen shook her arm, dislodging her friend's hand, and scooted down the pew, mumbling apologies to the families she had to step over. She pushed through the sanctuary doors and stood in the nearly empty foyer, her blood boiling. Rebecca and Ben were back from their honeymoon...was it too soon to call and invite them to lunch? They were both headed back to work tomorrow. Probably better to let them have one last day of vacation with just the two of them. Which left her where? She could head up to the balcony like she'd said, or she could just go home.

"Jen?" Paige slipped through the doors of the sanctuary and crossed the foyer. "You okay? I saw you leave..."

Jen sighed. She should smile and let it go. But...Paige might actually know something about Luc. "How well do you know Luc?"

Something flickered in Paige's eyes before she shook her head. "Not at all, really. From a few things Jackson said, Ben doesn't know him super well. Luc works onsite for several of their longer-term projects, when they're setting up agriculture or digging wells, those sorts of things. I'm not entirely sure how he came to be in the wedding party. I tried to explain to Rebecca that neither Amy nor I cared if you and Sara walked with the guys, but Rebecca wasn't having it. Why do you ask?"

"Sara. She's completely over the moon about the guy and she barely knows him. And he just seems...off."

"You're sure that's not jealousy speaking?"

Jen took a quick breath, an angry retort on her tongue, then stopped. Was it? Luc was handsome, certainly, but...smarmy. And that would be the right adjective even if her dating prospects weren't in the toilet. "Yeah. Yeah, I'm sure. I mean, okay, I'd like to have a guy who was interested in me. But not him. Throw in how fast Sara has jumped in with both feet and there's something off there."

"I wish I knew what to say. Don't let it ruin your friendship though, okay? You, Sara, and Rebecca have been friends a long time. Don't let that go over something like this."

Jen nodded. She'd try not to. But it might not be up to her.

"You want to come sit with me and Jackson?"

Why not? If she had to sit with a happy couple, it ought to at least be one that didn't make her physically ill. "Sure. Thanks."

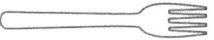

Jen turned away from her monitor and looked out her office window. The view was nothing to write home about—just another of Tyson Corner's tall office buildings—but at least it wasn't misbehaving code. There had to be something simple she was missing, but she'd been over the program twice already today. Why did it run in the test system but not when it got merged into production?

Her stomach rumbled. Maybe lunch would help her focus. She could take a few minutes and run across the street to the little deli. It wasn't amazing, but it'd fill the hole. She grabbed her wallet from her desk drawer. Maybe she'd see if some of the guys wanted to go. They might have a suggestion of where to look for the problem.

Tugging open her office door, she nearly bumped into David. "Hey."

He grinned. "Hey back. You on your way to lunch?"

"I am, actually. I was going to grab some of the guys and run over to Mia's."

David wrinkled his nose. "Do you have time for something better?"

"Not a Mia's fan?"

He shrugged. "It's fine. It's just the first place everyone thinks of and it gets old. It actually got me to bring my lunch for nearly a year. The first eight months I worked here, it was basically the only place I ate. After that, PB&J didn't sound so bad."

Jen chuckled. "All right. Where were you thinking?"

"Did you need to grab your friends? I don't want to interrupt something that's already set up."

"Nah. Grabbing them was an afterthought. I'm having trouble debugging something and was going to pick their brains. I can do that after lunch just as easily." And lunch with David was a more interesting prospect than the guys on her team. She took a deep breath, willing her heart to stop racing. Stopping by was a friendly gesture, nothing more. "How are things up in the teens?"

David gestured for her to go ahead of him. "Hectic. I had a handful of people come back from their vacation with new jobs."

"Ouch."

"Basically. So I've been running around trying to put out the fires that's causing. Today's the first day since New Year's that I realized it was time to eat before two. I'd intended to get down here sooner."

Jen caught one of her team members exaggeratedly batting his eye lashes by the coffee machine. She shot him a look even as her stomach clenched. Was the rumor mill going to be churning about her and David now? Did it matter if it did? "Oh?"

He stopped and punched the elevator button before turning to hold her gaze. "I'd like to get to know you better. I thought—hoped—you knew that."

"Why?" Heat flooded her face. She hadn't meant to say that out loud...even if it was a valid question. She cleared her throat. "I didn't mean...I'd like that too."

David frowned and opened his mouth. He snapped it shut as the elevator arrived and disgorged its passengers.

"So, where are we going? Not Mia's, obviously." Jen's laughter sounded forced to her ears, but it coaxed a smile from David.

"There's a little diner two blocks over if you have time. They can get crowded."

She'd heard of it, but never managed to get there. She didn't have anything pressing—well, beyond figuring out her code problem—scheduled for the afternoon. "Sounds good."

"David?" A stunning Korean woman, maybe in her late thirties, poked her head around the corner of the booth where they were sitting waiting for their server to have time to get to them.

"Ji. Hi." David flushed and smiled at Jen. "Jen, this is my sister, Ji-Yoon, Ji-Yoon, my friend Jen."

Jen extended her hand. Friend? Was that what they were? They were still getting to know one another. There was attraction—at least on her side—but wouldn't co-worker have been more accurate? "Pleasure to meet you."

"Have you eaten yet?" David looked at his sister.

"No. Just got here. It's more crowded than usual today, I'm going to end up sitting at the counter or getting my food to go, I think."

"Why don't you join us?" Jen scooted over, making room beside her instead of hogging the middle of the seat. Hopefully she'd say no, make her excuses. But offering was the polite thing to do and as ingrained as her mother could possibly have hoped.

"You're sure you don't mind?"

David gestured for his sister to sit. "If Jen doesn't, I don't."

"Of course not. It's just a friendly lunch and we have plenty of room." Jen's heart sank, her half-formed dreams of lunch turning into a date, or at least the offer of one, disappearing. "You work in the area?"

Ji nodded. "Two buildings away from David's office building."

Jen pictured it, her eyebrows lifting. That was where their primary competitor had their headquarters.

Ji grinned.

David chuckled. "You figured it out fast. But since my big sister was already taking over there, I figured I should apply somewhere else rather than ride her coat tails."

Ji shook her head. "I'll get you over there at some point, I know it. What about you? What do you do, Jen?"

"I'm a programmer a handful of floors below David. Our division does primarily supply chain solutions, generally not in the government space. I like knowing that we're helping some of the people and companies that put food on our tables—literally."

The server finally appeared and took their orders. The food was going to have to be amazing to make up for the lack of service. Jen didn't want to spend her whole afternoon at lunch, she did still have a program to debug. And she had to get home at close to the usual time or Tribble was going to have an accident. She really didn't want to have to pay for new carpet when she moved out of her apartment. Not that she had any immediate plans to do that, but that didn't mean she couldn't do her best to keep things pristine.

"So. Tell me how you and David met." Ji-Yoon crossed her arms on the table and glanced between Jen and David.

Jen shot David a look. Hadn't he said friends? Why was this starting to feel like an interrogation?

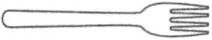

Jen tossed the ball for Tribble and the little dog bounded after it. She still didn't know what to think about bumping into David's sister at lunch. Was it really an accident? The woman seemed nice, but she'd had so many questions. They'd bounced from topic to topic with no rhyme or reason; she'd been off balance the whole meal.

"What was that even about, Trib?" Jen scrubbed the dog's head and picked up the slobbery ball and tossed it again. The dog tilted her head to the side and yipped before dashing after her toy.

"What are you doing out here? It's getting cold." Sara rubbed her arms and watched Tribble shaking the ball furiously before loping back toward Jen.

"Trib needed to play. I wanted the air. What brings you here?" Now that she was paying attention, it had gotten chilly. "Come on, Trib. Let's go inside."

Sara huffed out a breath. "I wanted to say I was sorry. About Sunday. I overreacted."

Jen slid open the glass door and waited while Trib and Sara went in. "Okay."

"Come on, Jen, don't be like that." Sara followed her into the kitchen.

Tribble lapped water noisily from her dish while Jen filled two mugs at the sink and stuck them in the microwave. "Tea?"

"Sure. You're really mad, aren't you?"

"No. I'm just...I don't know what I am. Afraid to be honest, I guess."

Sara frowned. "Don't, okay? Even if I don't like what you have to say, I still want to hear it. We're friends. That's what we do."

It used to be what they did, that was true. But it hadn't been the case where Luc was concerned. And that was part of the problem. "You promise not to bite my head off?"

Sara nodded.

"There's something off about Luc. He glommed on to you at the wedding and I've barely seen you since. If I went off with some random stranger, you'd be kicking down my door and wondering what kind of cult I'd gotten involved with."

Sara opened her mouth then snapped it shut.

Jen took the mugs out of the microwave and dropped teabags into them. She handed Sara one and carried the other into the living room, curling onto the sofa. "Do you really know him?"

"Of course I do. What do you think we do when we're together?"

Jen arched a brow.

"Please. Give me some credit. We talk."

"So you know about his childhood? His upbringing? What he does for a living?"

Sara shook her head. "Not...all of those things."

Jen took a sip. "How many siblings he has? What kind of church he goes to?"

"Do you know those things about David?"

"Yeah. And we're not even dating." Should she mention she'd met his sister? It would distract Sara, turn the conversation to her and away from Luc. Judging from the not-quite-scowl on her friend's face, maybe that was the right thing to do. At least she'd planted some food for thought. Hopefully. "I've even met his oldest sister."

"What? How'd that happen? I thought you weren't dating."

Jen sipped again, then set the mug down on the coffee table. "We aren't. But I think we might be headed that way. He came by at lunch and we ended up bumping into his sister while we were out."

"Mmmhmm. Convenient."

Jen's lips twitched. "That was my thought. Though if it was prearranged, he's got an amazing poker face. You would've thought they ran across each other on accident all the time. Which, to be fair, is possible. She works about a block from us, at one of the other big tech companies in Tyson's."

"Possible. Still fishy. How was it?"

"Strange. But okay, I guess. She's eleven years older than David, so forty? And she has everything together. Or at least it seems like it. I don't know if I made the grade. When we walked back after eating, he apologized, but she came across like a sister meeting a sibling's friend. Mostly. And then he had to run as soon as we got back because lunch took longer than we'd thought and he was late for a meeting."

"He hasn't called? Texted?"

Jen shook her head. That was the sticking point. Wouldn't he have touched base if he'd had a good time? Maybe asked her out on a real date? Taking it slow was one thing, but she'd read about glaciers that moved faster than this.

"So you text him. It's the twenty-first century. I'm pretty sure you're allowed to make the first move."

Jen winced. "I...can't do that."

Sara made a face. "You're so conventional."

Why did it always sound like a bad thing when Sara said it? She shrugged.

"Fine. But don't come crying to me when he never asks you out. Are you at least acting like you're interested in more? 'Cause if all you're doing is being sedate, friendly Jen, he's going to turn you into one of the guys and that'll be that." Sara pulled her phone out of her pocket, glanced at the display, and grinned. "I have to run. Keep me posted. Okay?"

Jen nodded. "Yeah, you too."

Sara paused, her hand on the doorknob. "Sorry. It's just that he's leaving—work stuff—tomorrow. He didn't know if he'd have time to see me tonight or not. But he got finished sooner than he thought. On the positive side, for you at least, he'll be gone several weeks. I'm sure I can work all your questions into email, 'k?"

"Sure." Jen forced a smile and made a shooing motion with her hand. "Go. Now that Ben and Rebecca are back and settling in, we'll have to arrange dinner. I'll text her and have her set it up."

"Great idea. 'Night."

The door clicked behind Sara as she hurried to her date with Luc. Jen frowned. Should she text David? Everyone did it...and he'd said they were friends. Was it already too late? If she had nothing to lose, would it hurt to check in with him? But if she was already one of the guys there wasn't a point to texting him in the first place. Who was she kidding? If he was interested beyond being friends, he would've said something. When it all came down to it, why would he be interested in her? She was nothing special.

6

David frowned at his phone. Should he text Jen? And say what? Lunch was fun—maybe it was too soon to have introduced her to Ji-Yoon, but his sister was persistent. And pushy. Today had bought him some time before she had to meet the whole crew. How much time...well, that would depend. But maybe he could stretch it 'til they'd been dating, in earnest, for a month or so. Of course, that would mean he asked her out on a real date, not just friendly lunches. Which sent him back to staring at his phone. He swiped it on and opened a new text, scrolling down to where Jen had put in her number. He smiled at the message she'd sent herself from his phone before tapping in his own message.

Enjoyed lunch today. Thanks for putting up with my sister.

He hovered his finger over send then finally poked it. He had to start the conversation somewhere. It was better to err on the side of friendly, wasn't it?

David set the phone down and pulled his laptop toward him. Better to keep working on his status report than sit and fret over how long it took for her to reply. He couldn't stop the occasional glance toward the device though. Was it too late at night? He tended to be a night owl, losing track of time once he got home. Maybe she was an early-to-bed kind of girl. Should he have waited and done it in the morning? His phone buzzed. He let out a breath he hadn't realized he was holding and snatched it.

Me too. Your sister is nice, if clearly older.

He laughed. Ji was definitely the eldest.

I always said it was like having two moms.

He hit send and glanced at his laptop. Who was he kidding? If she was up, he was going to text her. He shut the laptop and set it aside before swiveling to stretch out on the couch.

That's because you're the baby. Are you always up this late?

David winced. *Usually. Was it too late to text?*

He tapped the edge of the phone while he waited for her response. He should've waited.

No. I leave my phone in the kitchen when I go to bed. Was working on heading that way, but wasn't there yet. Night owl?

Guilty. Early riser?

Not really. Pretty much right in the middle. Normal person, you know?

David laughed. *Normal is overrated. Did you get your programming problem solved?*

As soon as he hit send, he kicked himself. Why'd he bring up work when there were so many other topics he could've hit upon? His phone buzzed again.

Mostly. Wasn't my code, found the issue. Now just have to convince teammate to fix his code. Or fix it and try to make it look like he did it that way to start out. Not sure which. Sometimes I hate being team lead.

The eternal struggle between getting it done right, fast, and helping the people you were responsible for improve and progress in their careers. *Ugh. No easy answer. Lunch tomorrow?*

Nice segue. Sure. Same time?

David scrolled through his mental to-do list. Most of his meetings weren't until the afternoon. *That should work. Anything you're hankering for?*

Hankering?

Heat crawled up his neck and across his cheeks. *Wasn't that the right word?*

Sure...but who says hankering?

Apparently I do. Question stands.

Not at the moment. Will ponder. Need sleep—see you tomorrow?

David chuckled. *You bet. Sweet dreams.*

He tucked his phone under his leg in case another text came and glared at his laptop. There was plenty to do, and he wasn't tired...might as well. With a sigh, he opened the lid and got back to work.

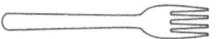

"Happy Tuesday." David leaned in the doorway to Jen's office and scanned the small space. She hadn't done much to personalize it. There were a couple of cartoons hanging off her monitor and a picture frame on her desk, but otherwise the walls were huge expanses of commercial white paint. Her white board had a few notes down one side, but the rest was clear and her markers were lined up in a neat row in the metal rail at the bottom. It wasn't hugely different from his own office, though he had a few more personal touches—maybe because he had a larger family? But if everyone was giving him photos of his nieces and nephews, he had to put them somewhere, didn't he? "Ready?"

"Yeah. Hang on." Jen clicked her mouse a few times and tapped her keyboard then reached into one of her desk drawers, pulling out the wallet she seemed to prefer to an actual purse. "Okay. So where are we headed?"

"Ever had Korean fried chicken?"

Her eyebrows lifted and she shook her head. "No. But it sounds interesting. What makes it different?"

"That's...hard to answer. Game to try?"

"Absolutely. We walking or do we have to drive?"

David glanced at his watch. He had meetings scheduled all afternoon, beginning at one. It was just barely eleven. "Either. What's your afternoon look like?"

"I really have to get this problem solved and something committed to the code repository by the close of business. I think I know what I'm doing, but..."

He laughed. "Nothing's guaranteed 'til you have it in the can. I get that. Why don't we drive?"

"How's your day been so far?" Jen smiled at him as he held the door into the elevator lobby open for her.

David winced. His morning had been horrible. Unfortunately, that wasn't unusual. "Fairly typical."

"You say that, but your face says otherwise." Jen stepped into the elevator. "Is it that bad?"

"It's not bad, really. Just...challenging, sometimes. But that's why I love it. Most days I can keep enough of a sense of humor to remember that. We're losing some key people. I thought I'd convinced one of them to stay, but he told me today he's still leaving. They're all, hopefully, going to finish their obligations. But you know how people are when they've mentally moved on. So I'm scrambling to fill spots so the contracts don't suffer." David stepped off the elevator and clicked the unlock button for his car doors. "I was up 'til almost one last night and that's probably going to be the new normal, at least for a while, since I have to be a bit more hands on during the transition. What'd you do last night?"

Jen chuckled and reached for her seatbelt as he closed her door and rounded the car to slide behind the steering wheel. "Played ball with my dog. Then Sara came over for a bit. You remember Sara?"

He nodded. "What kind of dog? I keep thinking I should get a pet—the apartment gets quiet at night. Some company would be nice."

"Tribble's a silky terrier."

"I'm not sure I'm familiar with that breed. Big? Little?"

Jen slipped her phone out of her pocket and swiped it several times. When they pulled into a parking spot in front of strip mall, she angled it so he could see.

"She's cute...but a girl dog."

She laughed. "Yeah, probably. But she's a sweetie."

"She does okay while you're at work?"

"Most days. If I don't run late. She's in a crate during the day, so it's not terrible if she has an accident, but I don't like to leave her stuck in there too long. Even if everyone says they enjoy it and feel secure, it seems mean somehow."

David nodded and held open the restaurant door. Familiar scents from his childhood reached him. Would Jen like it? He glanced over at her. She wasn't wrinkling her nose, at least. She stared up at the menu board above the counter. "Maybe I should think about a cat, instead."

"Rebecca has cats. She got them from a shelter in Arlington or Alexandria, I forget which. Either way, she could probably tell you all about cats. We always had dogs growing up. What's good?"

"Trust me?"

She gave him a long look before nodding. "All right."

He grinned and pointed to an empty table. "Why don't you sit, and I'll go order."

"Can I pay..."

"My treat."

Jen opened her mouth like she was going to argue, then closed it. "Thanks."

Cats and dogs. Could he have chosen a lamer topic of conversation? Work, maybe. Though she'd brought that up. Had he really been out of the dating pool for so long that he didn't know how to have a conversation with someone he was interested in? They'd gotten along so well at the wedding...what changed? The man in front of him finished ordering and stepped out of the way. The cashier, one of the owner's sons and a longtime family friend, grinned when David moved forward and greeted him in Korean.

"You haven't been here in ages, David, what brings you out?"

David glanced back over the restaurant. Jen had settled at a small two-person table in the front corner of the store-front window. "Helping a co-worker broaden her horizons."

The cashier looked around David and waggled his eyebrows. "Aha. I'll tell my mom to come out and take a look, then she can brag to your mom how she's already seen your new girlfriend. Being one up on your mom will make her day."

"No. We're not...she's not...wait. How do you know what my mom and your mom have been talking about?"

"Small restaurant, and there's nothing else to listen to in the kitchen before we open. If it helps any, they're both just relieved you're looking at someone again, after the Soo-Yi thing. Are you really changing churches?"

He was going to have to talk to his mother. Had she already told everyone in her ladies' group about this? He'd have to leave the church on principle. "I'm...thinking about it. Can I order before she thinks you don't actually serve food?"

"Of course. Sorry. I'm just glad mom's finally talking about someone other than me, even if it's only for a little while. I might go ahead and let my dad and grandfather arrange a meeting with someone. What can I get you?"

David rattled off his order, sticking to his favorites and dishes that had been well received by non-Koreans in the past. As he paid, he grappled with the idea of someone he knew agreeing to an arranged marriage. Well, he'd said meeting, but the understanding was there, wasn't it, that marriage would follow? It worked for some people...it was just absolutely not something he'd ever considered. He smiled at Jen as he sat across from her, his heart thundering in his chest. He liked her. She was intelligent, fun to talk to, and attractive. Maybe that should be bumped higher up in the list? It was certainly the first thing he'd noticed. There was no point in continuing to dance around the topic.

His mom's friend brought two trays over to their table. She gave him a knowing wink and patted his shoulder before scuttling back to the kitchen.

"You know the owners." It wasn't a question.

David nodded. "They go to our church. Mom and Mrs. Kim are good friends. Have been for years."

"That's neat." Jen looked down at the plates. "Tell me what everything is?"

"Can we pray first?"

Jen's eyebrows lifted, but she nodded.

David bowed his head and, after a moment, reached across and laid his hand on hers before saying a brief blessing over the food. After her quiet "Amen," he pointed to each item and named it and the major ingredients. She didn't turn her nose up at anything, at least. When he finished, he waited as she took a little of everything and put it on her plate before taking some for himself.

Before he could talk himself out of it, David cleared his throat. "Can I ask you something?"

She paused with her fork in the air. "Of course."

"Will you go out with me? On a real date. Friday?"

One corner of her mouth twitched up. "I'd like that."

"I need help."

David's sister opened the door wider and gestured for him to come in. His oldest niece, Madison, a precocious six, raced by, shrieking at the top of her lungs. Her little brother, Jeremy, zipped after her, hit the hall rug and slid into the wall before setting off a wail that could peel paint. "Welcome to bedlam."

"Maybe this is a bad time. I can call you later. Or something." Maybe he could ask a friend. He just hadn't wanted to get in to everything...deal with all the questions that would come. Ji already knew about Jen.

"Oh, no. You're here. Come on." Ji scooped up his sobbing nephew, cutting off the noise immediately. The four-year-old snuggled in and beamed a watery smile at David before reaching out.

David took the boy and grunted. "You're getting heavy."

"S'cause I'ma big boy."

"That's right." David kissed the boy's forehead before setting him down. "Are you going to let your sister get away with that?"

Jeremy shook his head vigorously and tore off in the direction his sister had disappeared. Madison's shriek pierced the temporary silence before Min's voice cut it off again.

"Aha, now their dad's on the case. He'll, hopefully, wrangle them into pajamas and start getting teeth brushed. What brings you out here on a weeknight?" Ji followed the hall to the kitchen and began rinsing dishes. The dishwasher was already open and half-loaded. He must have interrupted the chore.

David hopped onto a stool at the island and crossed his arms. "I asked her out."

"You asked her out. Jen? I thought you'd already asked her out."

"Lunch with a coworker isn't really the same thing. You know that. I asked her out on a date. A real one."

Ji grinned and closed the dishwasher, then rinsed her hands and dried them. "That's great. I liked her, by the way. A lot. So when's the date?"

"Friday. And I have no clue. I haven't been on a first date in...a long time. What do I do?"

"Seriously?" Ji shook her head and took two mugs out of the cabinet by the sink. She filled them with water and put them in the microwave. "Out of idle curiosity, why are you asking the sister who's been married fifteen years? I haven't been on a first date in a lot longer than you."

It was a fair point. But... "You're a girl. Don't you have stockpiles of date ideas stashed away somewhere?"

"I think at this point she prefers the term 'woman.'" Min pulled out the stool next to David and sat. "But if you do have a date idea stockpile somewhere, you should package it, sell it, and let me retire. I'll be a stay-at-home dad and even toss in vacuuming every now and then."

"Hey, man. Work's still bad?"

Min nodded.

David frowned. Min was a super programmer. He'd been doing a lot of proposal and grant writing lately. He was good at it, but apparently hated it. "I...might actually have a possible solution for you. I have a team-lead position that just opened up. There's still a decent amount of development involved, though you'd have management tasks, too. I'd need to make sure there wasn't a problem with you being my brother-in-law. Well...that's assuming you didn't have a problem with it first."

"Send me some details. I'm not immediately opposed. And at the least, maybe knowing I'm actively looking at another option will convince them to hold to their promise that this was temporary."

"You'd leave? Really?" Ji took the mugs out of the microwave and dropped teabags into them, putting one in front of David and the other in front of her husband. She got another mug down and filled it. "I can see if there are openings at my office. I haven't because I didn't think you'd even consider it."

"I might not have before today. They brought six new proposals and just dropped them on my desk. Do you have any idea how much time that's going to take? There's no way I'll get back to coding anytime soon. But that's enough about that. Who'd you ask out?"

David blew across the top of his tea before sipping. "Jen. Didn't Ji tell you about her?"

Min nodded. "Just making sure. What's wrong with dinner and a movie? If I recall, that was our first date. Things seem to have worked out okay."

Ji got her mug from the microwave and leaned against the island. "Or you can do dinner and something else. The weather's been pretty good, you could try a walk downtown. The Mall's pretty in the evening."

"I guess. I was hoping for something more, I don't know, creative? Unique? I want to make an impression."

"What about Shirlington? Good restaurants, nice place to stroll and window shop. And you could check the theater there and see if there's something live going on, comedy or some such. That's a little more interesting than sitting in a dark movie where you can't interact." Ji pulled the tea bag out of her mug and then out of David's. That was probably why it was starting to taste weird. He never remembered to take the things out.

"All right. I'll look into that. Thanks. Where are the minions? They've gotten quiet."

Min sighed and stood. "I should probably check on that. They're supposed to be getting ready for bed. They're probably playing. Good to see you, David. Let us know how the date goes."

David watched his brother-in-law take the stairs two at a time before turning back to his sister. "He doesn't really care about my date, does he?"

"Maybe he wants me to stop talking about how I wish you'd find a nice girl and settle down. I don't know." Ji shrugged and moved around to sit on the stool her husband had vacated.

David chuckled and took a long drink of tea. It was nice that his sister cared. Mostly. At least she wasn't pushy like his mom could be. Though again, it was hard to mind too much when you knew they just wanted the best for you. Soo-Yi had not been what's best though, and he'd known it long before he'd had to guts to break things off with her. She'd known it too—had told him as much. The pressure to get married though...it got heavy.

"What?"

"Nothing. It's nice that you care."

"Why wouldn't I care? I'm your older sister."

"But you were out of the house by the time I was what, ten? It's not like we were buddies growing up."

Ji slung her arm over David's shoulders. "Maybe not, but we are now. Right?"

He chuckled. "Sure. But only because your kids say I'm their favorite uncle."

She laughed and swatted his arm. "Go home. Don't stress the date too much. I have a feeling that whatever you decide is going to be great."

7

"Is that what you're wearing?" Sara dropped her backpack on Jen's couch and gestured for Jen to spin. "I guess it's not too bad."

Jen looked down at the black slacks and cheery yellow sweater. Casual but still dressy enough for just about anywhere. The peep-toe yellow heels were the perfect finish to the outfit. "What's wrong with it?"

"Nothing. It's hanging a little oddly though. Have you lost more weight?"

Jen lifted a shoulder. She'd dropped another couple of pounds but there was no point telling Sara that. She'd just start harping on her about how pretty she was and how there was no point in trying to lose weight. "These have always been a little roomy. So the outfit's okay?"

"Yeah. Any idea what you're doing?"

"Dinner. Then he said a surprise. So I'm not sure. That's why I'm trying to cover the bases with the outfit."

"Hmmm. You're not going to sleep with him on the first date, are you?"

"I'm not going to sleep with him on any date."

Sara waved her hand, dismissing Jen's objection. "You say that now. But when was the last time you had a serious boyfriend? College?"

Had it been that long? She'd dated, off and on, since then. But there'd never been anyone steady or exclusive. "I guess. Yeah. Why would that matter? Sex is for marriage. Period."

"Sure, in theory. But by the time you hit our age, it's just not realistic anymore. You need to let go of your prudish mindset and understand that guys aren't going to stick around if they're not getting what they want. Not that you just jump in right away. You have to make them wait a month or two, be sure you're in a committed, monogamous relationship."

Jen frowned at her friend. When had she become the kind of person who would think that, let alone say it? "The only relationship that meets those qualifications is marriage."

Sara shook her head. "You need to wake up and join the modern age. You'll see. Just remember, not too soon. You don't want him to think you're easy."

That much was true. "So...you and Luc..."

"Not yet. Soon, probably. Maybe when he's back. We'll see how things go. We haven't actually talked about being exclusive yet. That has to come first."

Jen needed to talk to Rebecca. Didn't the three of them share the same thought process? Well, obviously Sara didn't, but was Jen really that unusual? Some of the couples in the single's group thought that way, they made that clear by their actions. Weren't they the minority? Or was giving up on abstinence just what you did if you didn't happen to find your mate before you were twenty? This conversation was doing nothing to calm the butterflies in her stomach. She made a noncommittal sound.

"What time will he be here?"

Jen checked the time on the DVD player. "About forty-five minutes."

"That's probably my cue, then. I'll leave you to get Tribble ready for her evening alone. Have fun, okay? And try not to be too serious. It's a major failing of yours."

When Sara was gone, Jen sank into a chair. Too serious and a prude. Was it any wonder she hadn't had a date in longer than she cared to calculate? Was there anything worthwhile about her? A familiar heaviness began to settle over her, the weight centered in her chest. Tribble hopped up and settled on Jen's lap. She stroked the dog, her tense muscles loosening. After a few minutes, she grabbed her cell and punched in Rebecca's number.

"Hey, Jen. I was wondering when you were going to get around to calling me."

Jen smiled. Her friend always had a calming presence. Even on the phone. "I was trying to give you a few days to get settled. Plus, work's been really busy. How was your honeymoon?"

Rebecca laughed. "Really, really good. Is that why you called?"

"No. I'm going out with David tonight."

"David. David from the wedding David?"

"Yeah. And Sara was just here, helping, kinda, with my outfit and such..."

"Did she do the whole don't sleep with him right away but don't hold out too long speech?"

Jen sighed and closed her eyes. "She gave you the same one?"

"Only about twelve times. I...I've just been praying for her. I don't know what else to do. She's convinced that a relationship can't last without sex. She didn't used to be like that. I'm not sure what changed. I guess there are enough other people at church, people who you and I would think are solid Christians, who believe the same thing. So arguing with her is nearly impossible. Listen to me though, you don't have to buy that. Ben and I didn't. It wasn't always easy, but it was worth it."

"Okay. That helps."

"Have fun tonight. And let's do lunch sometime next week, the three of us."

"That's a deal. Thanks, Rebecca."

"Anytime."

"That was delicious. I've driven by here on 395 a number of times and always thought I should come by, see what there was, and just never made it happen."

David grinned. "I'm glad you liked it. Ice cream? There's a really neat place across the street and down a way."

Her mouth watered. Ice cream. Were there sweeter words in the English language? Of course, those words went along with an extra two hundred calories. On top of the largest meal she'd had in forever. "I don't think I have room."

The corners of David's mouth poked down, but he nodded. "All right. Want to walk a little, see if some space opens up?"

"Sure." Jen smiled. David held out his hand, a questioning look on his face. She slipped her hand into his. Tingles crept up her arm.

"You've really never been here? I think I first came with a group from church. The theater down at the end of the road was performing a musical that our music pastor at the time had helped write. They do a ton of locally-written stuff. Some of it's completely off the wall weird, but there are gems here and there."

"You like live theater?"

A flush crept across David's cheeks. "Yeah. Don't you?"

Jen shrugged. She didn't dislike it, but it hadn't ever crept into her top hundred things to do. "It's okay. Not something I go out of my way to see usually. You go to a lot of it?"

"Not as much as I'd like."

Silence stretched between them. Why was conversation so awkward tonight? When they'd gone to lunch they'd had lots to talk about. Jen cleared her throat. "So other than theater, what do you do with your free time?"

"There's a group of us from college and work who do stuff. Bike rides, hikes, volunteering for political campaigns, that kind of thing. Runs the gamut, really. Not everyone does everything, but there's usually something that sounds fun and takes up the day. It's getting a little trickier now that a lot of the guys are getting married.

Their wives, who hung around all the time when they were dating, suddenly have no interest in continuing. And the guys are caught in the middle. So things have been slowing down. When there's nothing that sounds interesting with the gang, I'll do more work—there's always work to do—or go for a bike ride on my own. Sundays are church, and then usually lunch with my family, which can turn into an all-day affair if I'm not careful. What about you?"

"Lately it's been me and my dog. My parents usually invite me over, and sometimes I'll do that. Then Rebecca, Sara, and I try to hit lunch after church on Sundays. The rest of the time I'll work out or do a puzzle. And...that sounds pathetic and lonely. It isn't, I promise." Most of the time, at least. She flashed a grin. There was no point in letting him realize just how pathetic she really was.

David slowed and peered in the window of the shop before turning back to her. "You sure you don't want ice cream?"

Someone pushed through the door, bringing the sugar-and-chocolate scented air with them. She could do an extra hour on the treadmill tomorrow. "That smells too good to pass up."

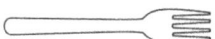

"Hey, Mom." Jen watched Tribble sniff the grass, looking for just the right place to do her business before bed. "Kinda late, isn't it?"

"I wanted to know how your date went. I wasn't sure when you'd get back, so I waited. You're still up, right?"

"Yeah. Taking Trib out for one last potty break."

"So?"

Jen sighed. She wanted to gush...but there hadn't been anything to gush about. They'd had better conversations at work during lunch. Even at Rebecca's wedding, when things had been in the awkward getting to know you stage it had felt less weird. The bright spot was holding his hand. She was attracted to him, no doubt.

But that wasn't the foundation for a lasting relationship. "I don't know. It was okay."

"Just okay? That's...not at all what I expected."

"Me either. I don't know, Mom, maybe I'm not cut out for a relationship. We were on our way to being friends, I think, and then this date...maybe we're better off leaving it alone. I can always use a friend." Tribble raced over and danced in a circle at Jen's feet. She bent down and scooped up her dog, carrying her back inside.

"Jennifer. Don't give up so easily. On yourself or on him."

"Yeah, I guess. I'd just like, for once, to have one of those dates that you read about. You know, the ones where you're swept off your feet and you end up feeling like you're the reason the sun came up that morning, that you're special. You know?"

"I do." Her mom sighed. "Sometimes you have to figure out what that looks like in real life though, baby. It's not likely to be what you read about in books. You have a good head on your shoulders, don't get sidetracked by fantasy. I love you."

"Love you too, Mom. Night."

Jen pushed 'end' on her phone and hooked it to the charger. Don't get sidetracked by fantasy. Easy as that. If fantasy never happened in real life, why were there so many books about it?

8

"I didn't expect to see you here, Jackson. No wedding plans to take care of?" David lightly punched Jackson's shoulder as he slipped between the closely packed tables and chairs in the local politician's office. Most of the chairs were occupied with young adults folding letters and stuffing them into envelopes.

"I wasn't expecting you, either. You've been absent from the political scene lately." Jackson grinned. "Have a seat and dive in. Heard you had a date last night. How'd that go?"

David's eyebrows lifted. "How'd you hear that?"

"Jen told Rebecca, Rebecca mentioned it at dinner last night at Season's Bounty. And you didn't answer the question."

David pulled out the chair next to Jackson and dragged a box of letters close. He skimmed one, flipping to the other side to ensure it was a single page, and then began to fold. "I'm not sure."

Jackson frowned. "What does that mean?"

"Dinner was good. But the longer we talked, the more stilted and awkward it got. At the end of the night, I was wondering if we had anything in common. Jen's someone I was beginning to consider a good friend, on top of the attraction I feel for her and now...I don't know, maybe I'm better off alone."

"Dude." Jackson shook his head and stuffed a letter into the envelope. "You like her, right?"

Hadn't they had this conversation already? "I thought I did."

"One bad date doesn't ruin a relationship. Give it another shot."

"You're speaking from experience here?"

Jackson winced. "Well...no. But it seems to me that Jen's someone worth fighting for."

David sighed. A day ago he would have agreed. That date though. "I don't know, man. Shouldn't it be easier than this?"

"Not if it's worthwhile."

David frowned and continued to stuff envelopes with donor letters. He wasn't afraid of hard work, but you had to start with something, didn't you? Something other than chemistry. Chemistry was easy. At least it was in his experience. Look at Soo-Yi. They'd had a ton of chemistry, had very nearly crossed lines that you couldn't go back over once you did. And yet they still were completely unsuited for each other. The chemistry was probably to blame for them staying together long after they both realized there wasn't anything more there. He didn't want to go down that path again.

"That's a long silence." Jackson stacked his filled envelopes in a box and tapped the edges flat.

"I don't know what to do."

"Pray about it." Jackson shrugged. "I know it sounds trite, but that's the first place to start, don't you think?"

"Yeah, I guess. Hey—since you're here. I was thinking of trying out some different churches, see if maybe there was someplace that fit me better. Do you like yours, would you recommend it?"

Jackson grinned. "I do and I would. Why don't you meet us there? We hit the ten o'clock service usually. There's a small group for singles and young couples after that we don't always get to, but it's nicer than the larger college and singles group. That one...is really only focused on finding dates. I think the leaders are trying to change things, but change takes time, I guess. Anyway, come with us and have lunch after."

"Yeah, all right." David took the small stack of stuffed envelopes and put them in his box before pulling another pile close.

"I've gotta run, Paige wants me to go look at cakes."

"Look at cakes? She's not catering your wedding?"

"See, that's what I thought, too. And her dad and the crew are handling the reception food, but I guess she doesn't trust them with the cake—wants a real bakery to do it."

David laughed. "Poor you, you have to go eat all kinds of cake."

Jackson shrugged. "I guess it's not so bad when you put it that way. See you in the morning."

David stared at the screen of his laptop. Was he really going to do this? Online dating. It was barely one step above having his grandparents find him a wife. Though at least this way he'd have a little say in things. He pictured Jen's face at the end of their date. Was there any chance for them? Not that filling out his profile would necessarily mean they couldn't go out. It just meant that he was open to other options.

Why did it feel like cheating?

His head dropped back and he stared at the popcorn ceiling. Why had people decided that was a good idea? Not that he was going to move out of this apartment simply because of the decor. He was right in the middle of things, his drive wasn't terrible...and why was he obsessing about his apartment when he needed to decide what he was doing?

He created an account and started on the profile. Who came up with these questions? His phone rang and he answered with one hand.

"Hello?"

"Hi, baby. Why are you answering your home phone on a Saturday night?"

His heart sank. Why hadn't he checked the caller ID? "Hi, Mom. There wasn't anything going on with anyone."

"Nothing?"

"Well, a couple of guys were headed downtown, but you know I'm not into the club scene." Which was an understatement. He enjoyed hanging out with his friends, and didn't mind the music. But all the drinking? Even from people who normally didn't drink much—there was something about being downtown at the hip spots that had them tossing back drinks and looking to hook up. They always regretted it in the morning. It got old being their weeping sounding board. And he couldn't dance worth beans.

"That makes me happy. But why aren't you out on a date? Ji said Jen is a sweet girl. You haven't asked her out?"

He sighed. "We went out last night. It...wasn't good. I don't know if there's anything there."

"Have I told you about my first date with your father?"

"I think so. Didn't you go to a church activity together?"

His mother laughed. "That was our second date. We'd gone out to dinner before. I ended up calling a taxi and wondering what I was thinking by agreeing to go out with him, by telling my parents that I would let them set me up."

Really? That was...not the story he'd grown up with. "Why didn't you ever say that before?"

"It's not my happiest memory. When I showed up at that church activity, your father nearly left. He was so mad. The way I'd left the date wasn't particularly kind. And his parents were blaming him for messing up, when it wasn't anything he'd done."

"What was it then?" Maybe his mom would have some insight. Even if it was sort of weird to be having this conversation with her.

"I don't know. I spent months trying to figure it out. But over time, we became friends and, after a while, when he asked me out again, I knew it was going to be better."

So. Not helpful after all. "I'm glad it worked out for you."

"I hear the unsaid 'even though it won't for me' on the end of your sentence. Don't give up so quickly. Have you been praying about it?"

Pray about it. The same advice Jackson had given him this morning. He was praying about it. There just didn't seem to be any answers coming. "Yeah. For all the good that does."

"Give it time. There's no hurry. Even if you feel like there is, there isn't. Wait for God's timing."

"Sure. Okay. Thanks, Mom."

"We'll see you tomorrow."

David winced. "Actually...I thought I'd try out another church tomorrow. I'm going with Jackson—you remember Jackson?"

"Of course I do. That's good, baby. Maybe branching out is just what you need. Don't stay up too late."

He hung up and shook his head, turning back to the dating website. Branching out. Maybe that's what he needed in all aspects of his life.

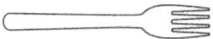

"So, what'd you think?" Jackson dropped into a chair next to David. The restaurant was crowded with families and a few scattered groups of young adults. And then there was the motley crew at their table. Jackson and Paige, Ben and Rebecca, and Sara. No Jen.

"I liked it. I'll give it another shot next week, maybe hit up a small group."

"Not too different?"

David shook his head. The songs were, mostly, the same. Just in English. The preaching was relevant and easy to follow. And best of all, he hadn't felt like everyone was looking at him, wondering when he was going to find a nice girl and settle down. Maybe no one at his church really did that, but it felt like it. Especially with more and more focus on Soo-Yi's upcoming marriage. Change was good. Still...where was Jen? He cleared his throat and aimed for casual. "Doesn't Jen usually sit with you all?"

Jackson smirked.

Rebecca slapped her menu down on the table. "Usually. I haven't been able to get a hold of her since Friday night. Have you, Sara?"

"Nope. And I was really hoping she'd want to hang out last night." Sara turned to Jackson. "Do you have any idea when Luc will be back in the area?"

Jackson shrugged. "Not really, no. He's in and out periodically, but you know he's based out of Martinique, right? Though that's a loose description anyway. He's barely ever there—to hear him tell it, it's just long enough to wash his clothes and kiss his mother. They keep him pretty busy."

Sara frowned, her lower lip poking out.

David straightened his silverware. He hadn't even tried to get in touch with Jen on Saturday. Even if the date hadn't been a disaster, he probably wouldn't have tried to get in touch the next day. Didn't that reek of desperation? He'd been half counting on her being at church today so he could get a feel for what she was thinking. Now...should he text her?

"I'm sure she's fine. You know she gets those moods, Sara. She probably saw you calling and knew you were going to try and get her to go do something downtown. That's hard to manage on the best of days. If she's cocooning, she just ignores the phone." Rebecca smiled. "But I'll text her this afternoon and set up a girls lunch later in the week."

Girls lunch? Just what he didn't need. She'd tell everyone what a horrible time they'd had and then there'd be no chance...of what? Wasn't there already no chance? That's why he'd gone ahead and paid his money to the online dating service last night. At least this one was, supposedly, just for Christians. David listened as the conversation swirled around him, moving away from Jen to the sermon and then plans for the week. He tried to smile at the right places and participate, but...was Jen okay?

After lunch, he hung back and snagged Rebecca as everyone was leaving. "You're not worried about Jen?"

She shook her head. "Nah. The thing you need to know about Jen is that she makes a lot of introverts look extroverted. She puts on a good front at work and church, but it takes a lot out of her. So every now and then, she pulls back and stays in. Guarantee she'll be fine at work tomorrow."

"Would knowing our date was kind of a disaster change any of that?"

Rebecca laughed then paused. "You're serious?"

David nodded.

"Hm. Let me have your number and if I get a hold of her this afternoon, I'll let you know."

He fished a business card out of his wallet and handed it to Rebecca. "Thanks."

9

Jen glanced at her cell as it buzzed yet again. Why couldn't people get the idea and leave her alone? She sighed and poked at the screen. Another text from Rebecca. Fine. She swiped the screen and punched a reply.

I'm fine. Let it go.

It wasn't a total lie.

Okay, fine, it was. Didn't mean Rebecca still shouldn't let it go. It wasn't as if there was anything wrong with taking a day, or two, to regroup.

She shouldn't need to regroup. It was one bad date. She'd had them before. Would probably have them again. Not like she was all that worth dating in the first place. Some people just figured it out faster than others. She scrubbed her hands over her face as her cell buzzed again.

Do I need to be worried?

Jen shook her head and picked up the phone, tapping Rebecca's photo and drumming her fingers on the table where the puzzle was just beginning to take shape.

"Hey." Rebecca was perky, as usual. Perkier, actually, than Jen had heard in a while. Marriage probably did that. If you could find someone who'd have you. Her friend was lucky.

"No, you don't need to worry."

"So...church?"

Jen sighed. "I took a day off, okay? It's not the end of the world."

"David seemed disappointed that you weren't there."

David? "Why was he there? He doesn't go there."

"Apparently he's trying out new places, looking to branch out. He liked it. And oh-so-subtly asked where you were."

Great. Perfect, in fact. Now she was going to have to find a new church. "I don't believe this."

"What do you mean? It's good, right?"

"Did he say anything about our date?" A long silence stretched between them. "He did. He said it was awful, didn't he?"

"He didn't use the word 'awful.'"

"Well, what word did he use?"

"Disaster?" Jen could hear the cringe in Rebecca's voice even after she hurried on. "But look, he's still asking about you, that's a good thing. How many guys wonder where someone is if they're not interested?"

"The ones who are making sure the nightmare they went out with isn't going to show up when they least expect it?"

Rebecca snickered. "Don't be an idiot. David's a nice guy. And the two of you are cute together. Just because you had a bumpy first—"

"Disastrous. Not bumpy. He wasn't wrong."

"Fine, disastrous first date doesn't mean it won't end up being something you laugh about with your grandchildren."

Jen scoffed. "That would imply he'll ask me out again. I'll bet you twenty bucks that doesn't happen."

"You're on."

Jen blinked. Seriously? She was taking the bet? Not that Jen hadn't been serious, but it was unlike Rebecca to be willing to risk any amount of money, let alone twenty dollars. "Great, I'll look forward to spending your money."

"I'm using my winnings on your wedding present." Rebecca paused and cleared her throat. "So you're okay?"

Jen sighed. "Yeah, I'm fine."

"Lunch on Wednesday?"

Wednesday. She could probably manage to look cheerful by then. "Sure. Usual place?"

"Yep. See you then."

Jen hit end and dropped the phone back on the table. Tribble growled quietly and paced to the sliding door. Already? Hadn't they just been out? She frowned at the time on her phone. How had it been three hours? "All right, Trib. Let's go for a little walk."

"Hey, some of the guys are going to lunch, you in?"

Jen looked up from her monitor and shook her head. "Not today, I brought something. I've been eating out a lot—too much—lately. Thanks though."

Braedon, one of her favorite coworkers hesitated in the doorway.

"Yeah?"

He frowned. "Are you okay? You've been...a little off this week."

Jen rubbed the back of her neck and forced a big smile. "I'm good. Just...life, you know? It's nothing. Sorry."

"Don't be. We—I—just wanted to be sure you were all right." Braedon knocked on the doorframe as he turned. "If you change your mind, we'll be downstairs."

Jen went back to work. She wasn't changing her mind. Lunch with Rebecca and Sara was tomorrow, and that was going to take everything she had in her. Besides, if she worked through lunch she could leave sooner, maybe take Tribble to the dog park for a little run.

"Hey."

She looked up, biting back a sigh when she saw David in her doorway. "Hi."

"You're a hard woman to find. Have time for lunch?"

"Sorry, no. I brought a sandwich." Jen hesitated. He was making an effort. And they could be friends. Maybe. "Rain check?"

"How about I go downstairs and grab a sub and bring it up? You've got to take a minute to actually eat."

Drat. She wasn't planning on eating her lunch, if you could call it that. She clicked on her calendar and fought a grin. "I have a meeting in ten."

David frowned. "Tomorrow?"

"Lunch with Rebecca."

He groaned. "I have lunch meetings Thursday and Friday."

"Don't worry about it. Thanks for stopping by."

"Jen...I..."

The phone on her desk rang, cutting him off. "I should grab this. See you around?"

He nodded. "Yeah. Sure. Later."

Jen grabbed the phone, her eyes following David as he turned down the hall. Why had he come? Did he really see any chance for them? Why hadn't he tried to get in touch before today? "This is Jen."

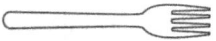

"Mom. What are you doing here?" Jen unlocked the door to her apartment and pushed it open for her mom. Tribble yipped from her crate. Jen dropped her bags by the door and headed into the kitchen to open the crate. Mom trailed behind her.

"Can't I stop by to see you?"

Jen's heart sank. "You can, of course, Mom, but you don't as a rule."

"You haven't returned my texts. Or calls. So I was curious...what's going on?"

"Come on, Trib." Jen patted her leg and slid past her mom toward the back door. "Nothing's going on. I've been busy."

"Too busy to tell me about your date?" Her mom glanced at the table as they walked past. "You've made a lot of progress."

Jen unlocked the door and opened it for the dog, who was dancing in place. Tribble dashed out to the grass and sniffed around for a second before doing her business. "You know I like puzzles. Isn't that why you bought it for me?"

Seconds ticked by. Jen avoided looking at her mom. Mom'd say her piece when she got to it and filling the silence only proved that there was something wrong. Words tugged at her tongue as jitters built in her belly. No. She wasn't unleashing the dam. She'd been down that route before, to no avail. Tribble switched to bouncing around the grassy patch, sniffing all the new smells that had blown around during the day.

"Are you taking your medicine?"

Heaviness settled in her chest and tears burned the back of her eyes. As if tiny white pills fixed everything, one-hundred percent of the time. She didn't bother to sigh. "Yes, Mom."

Her mom turned and held her gaze, eyes searching Jen's face. Finally, she gave a short nod. "Should you go back—"

"Mom, I'm fine, okay?" Jen forced a smile, opening her eyes wide so the light could hit them and make them look brighter than they were. Her mom had to believe her. The last thing she needed was her mom worrying.

"I just think you ought to consider going back to Dr. Mancini."

"Why, Mom? So he can tell me more about how I should cut you out of my life? That of course I'm depressed when I have a controlling and co-dependent mother? Or maybe that my father has improper feelings toward me and so my subconscious denial causes me to be unhappy? That's going to help me somehow?" Jen closed the door as Trib pranced in, then stalked into the kitchen and filled a glass at the sink. Her hands were shaking, blood was thundering in her ears. The easy answer. Always the easy answer. Go back to the shrink. Get more meds.

Her mother followed her, stopping in the doorway and leaning against the wall. Her voice was quiet, patronizing. "Honey. I just want you to be happy."

"I'm not *un*happy."

"Maybe happy's the wrong word. Not depressed. Is that better?"

"I'm okay. I'm sorry I didn't call you back. That doesn't mean I need an intervention. Maybe it just means I wanted some space."

Her mother's eyebrows shot up. "Well. Excuse me. I'll be going."

Jen closed her eyes, the weight in her chest getting heavier by the second. She should call her back. Stop her from leaving. Even if it wasn't wrong to need space, to feel sad. "Mom."

The steps stopped. Jen set the glass of water down and laced her fingers together, squeezing them to stop their trembling. She went into the living room. Her mom had her hand on the door, a frown etched into her features.

"Thank you for caring. I promise I'm all right. I love you."

"I love you, too. But I worry about you." Her mother gave a long, searching look. "I'm sorry that makes you angry."

Jen's shoulders fell. "I'm not angry, Mom. I...you don't need to worry."

"It's my job." Her mom pulled her into a hug. Jen forced her shoulders to relax like they normally would. No matter that the hug sent hot needles through her. "You're sure?"

Jen nodded. "I'm sure."

Her mother kissed Jen's forehead. "Call me if you need me."

"I will." Jen locked the door behind her mother, flipped off the lights, and crawled into bed. Tribble jumped up next to her and licked her face. The darkness pressed in on her until it was almost suffocating. She closed her eyes against the tears that wouldn't come.

_10_

David glanced at his phone. Jen was probably already gone, but there was no reason not to stop by on his way out and check. He hadn't seen her since Tuesday, though he'd looked when he had time. Maybe their schedules were at odds. They'd gone for years working at the same company without running into each other, why would that change? There was no reason to assume she was avoiding him.

He gathered his laptop and headed for the elevator. His cell rang.

"Hello?"

"What are you up to tonight?"

David checked the caller id. "Colin? Hey man. I'm gonna grab some takeout and do more work."

Colin chuckled. "You always were a workaholic. Got time for a friend?"

"You're in town?"

"Yeah. I'm doing some consulting for a little startup in Tyson's, remembered you're in Tyson's. The B&B is booked solid, so Rachel doesn't have any spare time tonight anyway, thought I'd see if you wanted to grab dinner."

It was better than a Friday night working. "Sounds good. Where?"

"You tell me."

David pursed his lips then rattled off directions before he ended the call and dropped the phone back into his pocket as the elevator arrived. His finger hovered over Jen's floor. She was probably already gone. The building emptied fast—and early—on

Fridays. Maybe he'd see her at church on Sunday. He punched the button for the garage.

Even with Friday traffic, it didn't take long to get to the small restaurant tucked into the back side of one of the many office buildings surrounding the mall. Colin was already waiting by the hostess stand. David grinned and extended his hand. "It's good to see you. I keep meaning to get out to Annapolis but..."

"Don't sweat it. I know how it goes."

"How many?" The hostess smiled.

"Two." David shook his head. "How's being a pub owner treating you? For that matter, how are you away on a Friday?"

Colin slipped into a chair at their table, set the menu aside and tented his fingers. "I finally found a fantastic manager, which makes being a pub owner considerably less stressful and gives me the chance to dabble with computer consulting here and there as the whim strikes. We've also found several more local musicians who are excited about taking a turn on the stage. So, while I get first dibs, I can take an evening or three off from that and share the wealth."

"Sounds...ideal." David fought a frown. Colin had had his setbacks. It was good that things were finally smoothing out. Why did it make his heart twist? Was he really that shallow that he couldn't be genuinely happy for a friend?

Colin angled his head to the side. "I take it things aren't that perfect in your world?"

Shallow and, apparently, transparent. David rubbed his temples. "Far from it. I'm losing three of my best people at the end of next week and only have a replacement for one—and not even the most important one. I'm going to end up absorbing their duties, or alienating some of the other team members as I share the work out, while we take the job listings outside. I was really praying there'd be someone who could transfer internally."

"That's it?" Colin paused as the server returned with glasses of water and took their orders. "Just work?"

How long had it been since he and Colin really had a heart-to-heart? Too long. Were they even that kind of friends anymore? Not that he had anyone else that he'd consider that type of friend, for all that he had a ton of friends. They were all superficial—people to hang out with, not people you bared your soul to. Colin...was both. Always had been. "There's this girl."

"Aha. I thought there might be."

David smiled. "No need to be smug."

"Of course there is. Us soon-to-be-married guys always are, or didn't you get that memo?" Colin sipped his water and lifted a finger as he swallowed. "Speaking of which, before we get into the deep details of your love life, you'll be my groomsman, right?"

"I...yeah, sure. You're sure?" David's thoughts scattered. "I thought you were having a small, family thing."

"We are. Rachel has her aunt standing up for her. We thought about just asking her new uncle to do the same, and then your name popped into my head."

"Cool. When?"

Colin cleared his throat. "So, it's a little hokey."

David drummed his fingers on the table and held his friend's gaze.

"Valentine's Day."

David snickered. "I guess you won't forget the date at least."

"I know, I know. But it's the soonest Siobhan, Rachel's aunt, could get tickets. And we want—need—it to be soon."

David nodded. They'd been settled in Annapolis over a year, engaged for at least half of that. "I'll be there. Just get me the details."

"Absolutely. Now, you can tell me about your mystery woman and then I'll get to meet her in February."

"I...don't think you'll get to meet her." David described their time at Ben and Rebecca's wedding, subsequent lunches, and disastrous date. "I signed up for an online dating site last week. Haven't seen anyone that I'm tempted to ask to coffee yet, but...it takes time. Right?"

"Have you at least talked to Jen since your date?"

"Just the once, when I'd been hoping to have lunch. Our schedules haven't meshed. It happens."

Colin shook his head. "I don't think so. She's avoiding you. Or you're avoiding her."

"I'm not." David snapped his mouth closed on the words. Maybe, just maybe, he could've done things differently and found time. Didn't she have to meet him half-way?

"If you say so." Colin leaned back as the server put his plate in front of him with a smile. "You're praying about it."

It wasn't a question. David stiffened. He was. Wasn't he? "Wouldn't our date have gone well if she's the woman God has for me?"

Colin laughed. "Sure. Just like Rachel fell into my arms with joy in Kinsale. You know better than that."

"I just don't think it's supposed to be this hard."

Was he being a wuss? David stared at the ceiling above his bed and listened to the creaks and ticks of the building in the night. Someone had their stereo on, loud enough that muffled thumps from the baseline worked their way through the walls. It wasn't that he was afraid of hard work. His job, his relationship with his family, ought to be proof of that. But Jen...where had things gone wrong?

"Jesus? Everyone keeps telling me to pray about it, and I have been—sort of. You know my heart. You know I want to find the woman You have for me. Is it Jen? Is that even possible? Or is it someone online whose profile I haven't run across yet? Can you make it clear to me, please? I'm not scared of a challenging relationship...well, maybe I am. I haven't had one before, so it could be that I have no idea what I'm saying. I probably don't. But if that's what You have for me, then it's what I want. I don't want something just because it's easy. Not if it's not from You." David flipped onto his stomach and let out a heavy sigh as he forced his eyes closed. "Please, Jesus. Give me wisdom. And some sleep. Amen."

11

"No, no, no. You bailed on us Wednesday, and last night, but you're not getting out of Saturday shopping. I'll be there in thirty minutes to pick you up. Be ready."

The line went dead. Jen frowned at her phone before setting it aside. Rebecca had been hounding her all week. Texts. Calls. The only thing she hadn't done was drop by. Looked like that was going to change. Thirty minutes? So much for a lazy day in pajamas, the one thing she'd been looking forward to all week. But she'd managed to smile and get through work, she could manage an afternoon with friends.

And if anyone asked, she'd just say she hated shopping. That much was true.

Jen dashed through a shower and threw on jeans and a light sweater. They were in the middle of the sneak peek of spring that always seemed to happen at the end of January in D.C. But it was still chilly enough. And the sweater hid the fact that she hadn't eaten much this week, leaving her jeans baggy at the waist. Where was her belt? She dug through the pile of clothes and shoes on the floor of her closet—she needed to get that all picked up—and finally emerged with a brown leather belt. Tribble danced around her feet as she carried her shoes into the living room and checked the clock. Ten minutes to spare.

"Come on, girl, let's go outside." Jen opened the sliding door and stepped across the concrete patio to the grassy spot where Tribble was busy sniffing around. When the dog was finished, they went back inside and Jen double-checked the locks. She slipped her phone into her small purse and dropped onto the couch to wait. She should've tried harder to get out of this. Her energy had already leeched out of her bones. What would be better than stretching out, dragging a blanket up over her, and zoning out in front of the television for the day? Napping off and on, and just generally not dealing with life.

Someone banged on the door. Jen sighed, forced a smile, and pulled herself up.

"You're ready. I figured I'd have to push you into the shower and...no makeup?"

Jen shrugged. "It's Saturday. We're shopping. Do I need to be self-conscious?"

"No. I'm just not used to you going out without at least foundation on. If you're good, I'm good. Ready?"

Not really. She cast a longing look at the couch where Tribble was curled up. "I guess. What are we shopping for?"

Rebecca looked at her like she'd grown an extra head. "Whatever we find. Are you sure you're okay?"

"'Course. Just wanted to be sure there wasn't something specific on your list."

"Nope. I'm simply looking forward to a day with my friends."

"Because married life is so boring you already need to get away?"

Rebecca snickered and bumped Jen's shoulder. "Nope. Come on. Sara's meeting us there."

Oh goody. Jen followed Rebecca out the front door. "Bye, Trib. Be good."

In the car, Jen snapped her seatbelt into place.

"How was your week? Any hot lunch dates other than the one you bailed on, leaving me to hear Sara rhapsodize about Luc all by myself? You owe me for that, by the way."

"I don't see how. I had to deal with it while you were on your honeymoon. Did she tell you she tried to bring him on a Sunday lunch?"

Rebecca nodded. "She mentioned it. Seems like as the days go by with him out of town, sanity is returning."

That was good at least. Maybe the day wouldn't be full of Sara's incoherent ramblings about destiny and love at first sight.

"You didn't answer my question. I take it that means no, you didn't have lunch with David this week?"

"It was a busy week. If I didn't have lunch with you, why would I go out with him? He doesn't even like me."

Rebecca glanced over, a frown etched into her features. "Yes, he does. I don't know why you say that."

"How would you even know? One conversation at church last week where he asked where I was? I'm telling you, that doesn't mean anything. At best, he was being nice." Jen's money was on him making sure she wasn't going to show up.

Rebecca shrugged. "I just know these things."

Jen scoffed. Time to change the subject. "Tell me about St. Thomas."

Tribble greeted her at the door with a shoe in her mouth.

Jen sighed. She should've put the dog in her crate. All the trainers said that dogs like their crates, but it killed her to do it. And yet, faced with the alternative...dumb dog. "Tribble. No."

Tribble dropped the shoe and pranced off toward the sliding door. Clearly she wasn't scarred for life. Or at all. Jen hooked the shoe with one finger, grimacing at the slime that dripped down her hand. Ugh. She dropped it in the kitchen trash before unlocking the slider to let Tribble out. Her day with Rebecca and Sara had been nice. Surprisingly. After the first hour, she hadn't needed to remind herself to smile, and for a while, at least, the weight on her chest had lifted.

Jen took out her phone as it started to ring, one eye on Tribble happily bounding about in the small grassy area. "Hello?"

"Hi, Jen? It's David."

Her stomach clenched. "Hi."

"I'm sorry we missed each other all week. I was really hoping we'd be able to do lunch at least once."

Jen frowned. That couldn't possibly be true. Except...why would he call just to lie to her? It'd be easier to say nothing and fade away. Isn't that what most people did these days? So maybe there was a little truth there? "Me too. But I know how it gets."

"I...were you planning to go to church tomorrow? Your usual church?"

Rebecca had asked her the same thing. She honestly hadn't decided one way or the other. Most of her wanted to stay home and take advantage of the quiet, avoid the effort that convincing people you were happy required. And if she did her Bible study and spent extra time praying, wasn't that basically the same thing? "Probably."

"Cool. Would it be okay if I sat with you?"

Jen patted her leg, calling Tribble to her. She leaned down and scooped up the pup when she got close enough and headed back inside. "Yeah. Sure. I usually sit with Sara and Rebecca. Which of course means Ben, Jackson, and Paige now, too. And Zach, if he's making the trek out of the city."

He chuckled. "So I'll see you tomorrow?"

"Sounds like it."

"Looking forward to it. 'Night."

"Night." Jen hit end and shook her head. That was...weird. Weird was the only possible word to describe that conversation. It wasn't as if she'd get up and move to a different pew if he came and sat down with them. So why would he ask if it was okay? It made it sound like he was coming to church again to see her. But that wasn't possible. After their date...was there even a chance they could stay friends?

Her heart ached. She wanted to stay friends. She wanted more than that, if she was honest with herself. He was cute, interesting, and he made her laugh. Plus, there was no denying they had chemistry. What went wrong on their date? It was her. It had to be. Heaviness settled over her, pushing away any of the last strains of joy she'd found shopping with her friends. She scooped dry food into Tribble's bowl and went back out to the living room. Laying down on the couch, she dragged a blanket over her and clicked on the TV.

Looks like she'd get that binge watching in after all. *Why, God? Why did you make me this way? Why couldn't you make me someone worth loving?*

David jingled the change in his pocket. She wasn't here yet. Why wasn't she here? Everyone else was already in the sanctuary. He'd gone in to put his Bible down, to save a spot as much as to know where to sit. But no Jen. She'd said she was coming. Strains of music from the worship band blasted through the door as a group of people opened it and filed in. He should just go sit. She'd either come or not.

He wanted to see her.

David tugged open the door to the sanctuary and made his way to the pew where everyone was sitting. He picked up his Bible and looked back toward the foyer before taking a seat.

"Is she usually late?"

Sara, seated next to him, shook her head. "She's usually the first one here. Did you text her?"

"I didn't want to seem like I was nagging."

Sara scoffed. "It's not nagging, it's interest. Text her. If she doesn't appreciate it, I'll kick her."

David slipped his cell out of his pocket.

"Sorry. I know I'm late." Jen slid into the pew, brushing past David and leaving a swath of tingles behind her. Sara scooted over, making space for Jen to sit next to him.

David put his phone away. "I'm glad you made it."

Pink colored her cheeks and she looked down.

"Let's stand and praise the Lord together." The worship leader stepped back and nodded to the band who kicked the music into high gear. Words flashed onto the screens on either side of the stage.

David stood, watching Jen out of the side of his eye. She was pale—other than the blush that still tinged her cheeks—and there were dark circles under her eyes. What had caused those? His fingers itched to twine with hers. That would be too forward. Somewhere in the middle of the night, he'd made the decision that Jen was worth pursuing. He just had to figure out the right tactic. It seemed like the usual method, the straightforward method, wasn't going to work as well with Jen as it did with other women. Not that he was particularly adept with other women, but still.

He struggled through the service, his mind constantly wandering to the woman beside him. She took notes furiously through the sermon. And when she wasn't writing, she was drawing interlocking swirls along the side of her page. Did she even realize she doodled, or was it just reflex? David jotted down the scripture references and a few points, but he was going to have to spend time this afternoon reading them again, maybe replaying the podcast, if he was going to get anything more from the service than confirmation that he found Jen attractive and wanted to know her better.

As the recessional started, David shifted to face Jen. "Lunch?"

"Sure." Jen turned to include Sara in the conversation. "We're doing lunch, right?"

"Think so. Lunch, right guys?" Sara raised her voice over the din of families filing out of the church.

David fought a frown. He hadn't intended it to be a group exercise. But...maybe it was for the best. He needed to figure out a plan.

David finished the email to his friend in HR and hit send. Hopefully the woman down on six would be a good fit for the team lead job. She looked good on paper. Who did he know on six? He drummed his fingers on his desk, then smiled and opened a new email. He tapped out a quick question to a guy he'd worked with on a proposal last year. With any luck, he'd know the woman and give the straight scoop on why she was looking for an internal transfer. Her current contract wasn't up. That didn't necessarily mean something bad. But it was better to know for sure going in. He checked the time on his screen. It might be a little early, but if he went down now, Jen couldn't claim she'd already eaten. He locked his machine, tucked his phone in his pocket, and left his office.

"David. Just the man I was looking for."

David winced as his boss hailed him. "Kurt. What's up?"

"Any progress filling your vacancies yet?"

"I think so. Got a lead for an internal just this morning. I'm hoping I can meet with her today, tomorrow at the latest. It'd be nice to have time for an actual transition if we can swing it."

"Good. That's good." Kurt nodded. "I'm going to need you to help with a new proposal effort. I'll send you the information this afternoon, but clear some space for that, okay?"

David nodded, his stomach sinking. Proposals. His very least favorite thing. They were necessary, he got that. But still, what a waste of time. Kurt had to know how much he detested them. Seemed like the man took great pleasure assigning them to him. "Will do."

"Great. Have a good lunch."

"Thanks." He stabbed the elevator button. That had been relatively painless at least. And it hadn't taken too long. Maybe he still had a chance to catch Jen. He entered the elevator with a nod to the handful of folks already on board, and pressed Jen's floor, his lips curving into a smile. He'd spent yesterday afternoon and evening praying and planning. It was time to put the plan into action.

When it stopped on Jen's floor, David stepped off the elevator and took a deep breath. *Please, Jesus, let this be the right thing. And if it's not—if Jen isn't who you have for me—make it clear.* He swiped his badge and went through the door from the elevator lobby into the maze of offices, nodding to the few faces that were becoming familiar from his visits to Jen's. When he got to her office, her door was mostly closed, so he knocked once and pushed it open a tad more.

Frowning, Jen looked up, the handset of her phone held to her ear. She rolled her eyes and lifted a finger, then pointed to one of the chairs in front of her desk and mouthed, "I'll be done soon I hope."

David grinned and sat, slipping his phone out of his pocket and opening his email. His boss had, in fact, emailed the proposal information. He scanned the introductory material. It was certainly something they could deliver, but they'd worked with subcontractors who were better at it in the past. He kept scrolling. Aha. This was basically an excuse to partner with one of Kurt's favorite companies, do relatively little work, and get the pat on the back for bringing in some cash. At least it wouldn't take long to throw together.

"Yeah...yeah okay. Right. By the end of the day. 'Bye." Jen hung up the phone and pinched the bridge of her nose.

"Uh-oh."

She sighed. "Not really a full-on uh-oh, but yeah, close. The customer let one of their programmers 'fix' something. And now, as you'd expect, nothing is working. So regardless of the fact we're supposed to deliver the next iteration on Friday, we're supposed to stop everything and get it working again."

David winced. "They probably do need it to work..."

"I know, I know. But if they'd just kept their programmers out of things, this wouldn't have happened in the first place." Jen's fingers moved rapidly over her keyboard for several seconds. She moved the mouse and then leaned back. "I think Marcus can probably fix it and he's not making any progress with his assignment anyway, so...that's not what brought you down here."

He laughed. "No. I was wondering if you had time for lunch. But...maybe you're too busy?"

Jen gave him a long look. "What's going on, David?"

"Lunch? Putting food into our bodies so that we're able to stay awake through the afternoon?"

"That's not what I meant and you know it."

He shrugged. "I like you. I enjoy spending time with you. And I like to eat."

Jen shook her head. "Why?"

Did she really have such a low opinion of herself? That wasn't the first time she'd asked something like that. Maybe the best course of action was to play it off. "'Cause I'm hungry. You in?"

"I guess. A girl's gotta eat, right?" She reached into a desk drawer and pulled out her purse. "Where to?"

Victory. David grinned. "How much time do you have?"

"Whatever. I need to give Marcus a sporting chance at fixing the problem before I follow up with him. If I'm back too soon, I know I'm going to go ask."

"Like Vietnamese food?"

Jen blinked. "I'm not sure I've ever had it."

"Then you're in for a treat."

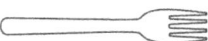

"Two visits in a month, I'm not sure what the world is coming to." Ji laughed as she opened the door and stepped out of the way.

"It was either ask you or Mom...or I could ask some of my guy friends, and I'm pretty sure, given their track record, that wouldn't be the right choice."

"Ah. Woman questions. I thought you understood all that."

David jammed his elbow into Ji's ribs. "Don't be weird. This is serious."

Min came down the stairs. "Stop manhandling my wife, please. Even if she is your sister. What brings you out this way again so soon?"

"It's not like I never visit." David frowned. Maybe he wouldn't usually come on a Monday night, but he spent time with his siblings. He loved his nieces and nephews. All of them. He crossed his arms. "Should I go? I can call and ask Mom."

"Touchy, touchy. Must be serious." Min grinned. "I'll go put the kettle on."

He didn't want tea. He jammed his hands in his pockets. Maybe this had been a bad idea after all.

Ji touched his arm. "You okay?"

He nodded. "I am. I've been praying about Jen...I really feel like she's who I'm supposed to be with."

"Oh, that's great. I liked her a lot. When can we have the two of you over?"

"It's going to be a little trickier than that, I think. I'm not sure she's as interested in me as I am in her. Or, if she's interested, she doesn't understand why I am. There's something there, and that's what I wanted a woman's take on."

"Why do you say that?" Ji gestured to one of the stools at the kitchen island and turned to take the now whistling tea kettle off the stove. She took down two mugs—Min had disappeared again—and poured the steaming water over the tea bags she dropped in.

"I drink more tea at your house than anywhere else."

Ji smiled and pushed a mug toward him before taking the seat next to him. "So?"

He cupped his hands around the mug. The heat was nice. And the faint traces of mint wafting up on the steam was pleasant. "A couple of times now when I've said that I liked her or that I wanted to spend time with her, get to know her better, her default reaction was 'why'?"

"Hmm." Ji sipped her tea and wrinkled her nose. After emptying a sugar packet into it and giving a quick stir with her finger tip, she sipped again. With a nod, she pushed the sugar packets toward David. "Lots of women struggle with self-esteem. Though I don't know any who are as upfront about it. It's one of the things I worry about as the mother of a little girl. Everywhere you look there are messages that you have to look a certain way, act a certain way, *be* a certain way if you're a woman. And most of those messages are wrong. But the church doesn't necessarily do anything to combat it. We hear about the woman in Proverbs thirty-one and get an even bigger complex. In addition to being sexy and always having our not-quite-size-one bodies perfectly put together, we're supposed to run a business and flawlessly manage our families at the same time. It's easy to feel you don't—can't—measure up. And if you spend too long feeling that way or, worse, having your failings pointed out to you, you start to believe it."

Nodding slowly, David reached for a sugar packet and dumped it in his tea. "Is there any way to help? I like her, Ji. It bothers me to hear her talk like that about herself. And it makes me wonder what madness she must tell herself. I mean, if she's not able to understand why someone would want to go out with her, what lies does she believe?"

"Just keep saying the things you are. Let her know she's special. Without coming across as patronizing."

David laughed. "That's the trick, isn't it?"

Ji nodded. "Yep. I suspect she's important enough to you that you'll manage."

Jen leaned her head back and let out a loud sigh. The delivery was done and, if she was any judge of facial expressions, the customers were delighted with the new additions. The demo had gone better than usual, without the obnoxious questions from the two in-house programmers who resented the fact that their company had gone outside to have the software developed. Maybe they were properly chastised after the "fixing it" debacle earlier in the week. Whatever it was, their silence had been the best part of the demo. Well, that and the software working like it was supposed to. That was always a bonus. Another hour or so wrapping up a few final details and she'd be off.

"Knock knock?" David poked his head through the door and grinned. "How'd it go?"

"It went really well." Jen smiled. David had stopped by every day this week. He couldn't always swing lunch, but when that was the case, he'd brought a candy bar or a printed out comic that had made him smile, so he'd said he wanted to share them with her. Nothing huge, just little things that left her warm inside. She could almost believe he truly meant it when he said he liked her. "I need to make a few changes to the documentation—I noticed in the demo it wasn't working exactly like it was written up. After that, I'm looking at a gloriously worry-free weekend."

"Excellent. Then these aren't misplaced." David brought a bouquet of bright pink and purple gerbera daisies from behind his back with a flourish. "I figured they could be either celebratory flowers or a consolation. I have to admit I'm glad they're the former."

Her stomach did a lazy flip as warmth spread through her. "Oh...those are beautiful. So cheery. Thank you."

"You're welcome. Congratulations on a successful delivery. You free for dinner?"

Jen's shoulders slumped. "I wish I was. I promised Rebecca that I'd go to Season's Bounty with her and Ben. Jackson will be there—he's there nearly every Friday...you want to come?"

"You don't think they'd mind?"

"I don't know why they would. We might have to squeeze if Zach and Amy show up, but Paige never seems to mind dragging in extra chairs." Would he come? Jen held her breath and tried to read his expression.

"Okay. I'd like that. What time?"

Jen checked the clock on her monitor. "After I finish up here, I have to run home and let Tribble out for a few minutes, then get her dinner. So I probably won't be there 'til seven at the earliest."

"Can I pick you up? We could save on parking and gas."

That made it feel more like a date. Except...it wasn't, really. She'd asked him along to an already-planned group activity. That couldn't be considered a date. And even if it could, so what? He said he liked her. She dreamed about him every night. Heat crawled up her neck and across her cheeks. "Okay. Six-thirty?"

"Sounds good." David nodded toward the flowers. "Those should be fine without a vase 'til you get them home. They have those little water things on their stems."

He thought of everything. She couldn't stop the smile, though she probably looked like an idiot. "'K. See you in a bit."

With a wave, he disappeared back down the hall. Jen counted to three in her head then picked up the flowers and buried her nose in them. Such a sweet guy. She couldn't possibly deserve him.

David pushed open the swinging door into the kitchen and gestured for Jen to go ahead of him. The noise, heat, and amazing smells slammed into her. Her mouth watered, even as she shrank from the clanging of pans.

"Hey, you made it." Rebecca grinned and scooted closer to Ben to make room on the booth next to her. "David? Come on, sit down."

Jackson looked up from the crossword puzzle he was working. "Hey, guys. Hang on, I'll switch sides and sit with Ben and Rebecca, that way you two can sit next to each other."

"You don't have—" Jen stopped as Jackson slid out of the booth. "Thanks. Is Sara coming?"

Rebecca shook her head, frowning. "No. I guess Luc's back in town."

"Sorry." Ben rubbed the back of his neck. "I didn't realize he'd be back so soon. I'm starting to regret having him fill in at the wedding."

Jen slid into the seat, smiling as David sat beside her, close enough that their legs brushed if she moved. Tingles worked their way up and down her right side. "If she keeps to her usual pattern, this'll burn out before much longer. It's been a month."

Rebecca snickered. "That's mean. True. But still mean."

Was it? Jen shrugged. "Just calling it like I see it. I get tired of picking up the pieces of her heart, you know?"

"Yeah." Rebecca reached across the table and patted Jen's hand. "I know that job mostly falls to you. Not sure why. Maybe I'm not as understanding as I should be."

Paige hurried over with a loaded platter and some smaller plates. She slid them onto the table and flashed a harried grin. "Hey, guys. Gotta run, but let me know what you think of this. It's an experiment. I think it's good. The guys on the line disagree. So you're the deciding vote."

"What is..." Jackson frowned at Paige's retreating form. "I guess we just eat it and find out? She needs to can every single one of those guys and find a new group. They've been giving her fits for the last week. I don't know what the problem is, but I'm ready to go in and knock some heads together."

David winced. "That's not good. Especially not with wedding stress that's gotta be ramping up. You're what, seven weeks away?"

Jackson nodded. "Invitations went in the mail today. A week late, but it is what it is. I can't quite get her to see it that way."

"It's her wedding, of course she doesn't." Jen shook her head. Were men really that clueless? You'd think in today's world, where wedding shows were a dime a dozen, guys would've clued in to the fact that weddings meant a lot to the women involved. Even if you didn't go crazy and break the bank, it was an important day.

Rebecca laughed. "He's not going to understand. He's a guy. I have it on good authority that most guys only care about what comes after."

"Hey. That's not what I said." Ben's cheeks flushed a dark red.

David and Jackson laughed.

Jen snickered.

Rebecca kissed his cheek. "Aw, honey, you're blushing."

Ben mumbled something under his breath.

Jen looked at the plate of thin rounds of toasted bread covered in some sort of paste. Paté? Wasn't that liver? Her stomach clenched. Don't judge before you try it. She slid one onto a plate and poked the paste with a finger then sniffed it. Garlic, for sure, and...olives? Where would Paige get olives locally? She licked the tiny bit of paste off her finger and tapped her lips together. It wasn't bad. A little strange though.

"Well?"

Jen started. David had been watching her? Heat spread across her cheeks. "Um. It's interesting?"

David arched a brow. "Interesting. What is it?"

"I don't know." Jen took a deep breath, picked up the toast, and took a bite. "Something with garlic in it. I thought olives, at first, but I don't think olives grow in the U.S. Mushrooms, maybe?"

Jackson fiddled with his phone for a moment then looked up. "According to the vast knowledge collected on the Internet, olives can grow in the U.S., but only in California, Hawaii, and Florida."

"So, not olives." Jen took another nibble. "It's still not bad."

The kitchen door swung in as Zach and Amy passed through it.

"Hey, man. Glad you could make it." Ben leaned across the table to bump fists with Zach. "Good to see you, too, Amy."

Amy laughed. "I see where I fall in the overall scheme of things. It's great to see all of you guys. I was so glad when Zach moved to D.C. I don't think it occurred to me how much we'd miss the gang."

Jackson stood. "You sit here, I'll go grab a chair and Zach can sit in that. I'll squish in with David and Jen."

Jen shook her head. If they were going to keep gathering like this, they'd need a bigger table. Or to sit out front or something. Not that they'd make a routine of this. Everyone was getting married and moving. Kids would be next. Then no one would have time to go out. And she'd be left by the wayside. Which was fine. It was. She had her dog. And her puzzles. Really, that was for the best anyway. It wasn't as if she had much to offer.

David scooted closer as Jackson returned with a chair and sat. Sparks sizzled up and down her side. She shot a glance his way. If he noticed, he didn't show it. He leaned over, his voice low. "I like how you're open to trying new things, and that you found something positive to say about it even when you weren't sure what it was."

"Thanks. I think?" Jen drew her eyebrows together. It sounded like a compliment, and yet...it was odd. "You going to try it or just stare at it?"

David chuckled and took a bite. "Better?"

Jen nodded.

Amy reached for the plate and took a big bite from the piece she snagged. She blinked rapidly as she began to chew. "What is this?"

Everyone around the table chuckled. Finally, Rebecca shrugged. "Paige was in a rush, so we don't actually know."

"It's...interesting." Amy swallowed and eyed the rest of the bread in her hand.

"That's what I said." Jen grinned. "How's school treating you, now that the big holiday program is over?"

Amy rolled her eyes. "Like that frees up any time."

Zach laughed. "It would've, if you hadn't suggested the whole greenhouse-slash-community garden project. Now we're spending every waking moment getting that set up."

"It's worth it though. Have you seen how excited these kids are? And the families that come on Saturday? We'll be done in no time. It's going to be great for the neighborhood." Amy frowned at the platter before taking another round of bread and biting into it.

"True. Though that actually factors in to why we're here. Anyone interested in helping us plant either this weekend or next? The greenhouse is ready and waiting for seedlings." Zach took the last bread round and bit into it. "Mmm. This is delicious."

"You like it?" Paige shuffled over, her arms laden with two huge platters. She set them down and perched on Jackson's knee. "It's so great to see you all. We haven't had a group this big in a long time. What's new?"

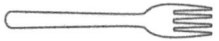

"Thanks for inviting me tonight."

Jen fumbled the key to her apartment. He was standing so close it was as if little zips of electricity were sparking off him. "Thanks for driving. Parking down there on Fridays is always such a nightmare."

"My pleasure." David lifted her chin and held her gaze.

Jen's hand froze on the knob. Was he going to kiss her? Her tongue darted between her lips. Did she even want him to? Well, of course she wanted him to, but was it a good idea? He couldn't possibly be serious about liking her. Could he? She cleared her throat and looked away.

"Jen?"

Her gaze darted back. "Yeah?"

"You're amazing and very special to me. I'll see you Sunday?"

She blinked once and nodded.

He grinned and reached down, turned the doorknob, and pushed open her door. "Okay. Have a good night."

"You too." Jen closed the door behind her and sagged against it. Special. Amazing. But not kissable. Okay, maybe it was too soon for that. Had he at least wanted to? No way to know. Past experience would suggest he probably didn't. But...David was different. The things he said and did...maybe she was good enough?

It didn't seem possible. David was smart, good looking, and a solid Christian. What could he possibly see in her? She was just a nerdy girl who struggled in large groups—and, if she was honest, in small ones too. There was nothing special about her. Why would he say there was?

Her shoulders slumped as she locked the door and headed to Tribble's crate to let her out. "Come on, girl. Let's go potty one last time."

She opened the sliding glass door and let the dog run out to the little patch of green. What would it be like to be cherished? To have someone believe you were worthwhile—believe so strongly that you might even believe it yourself? She scoffed. Like that was going to happen in this lifetime. People just didn't see her that way.

Tribble dashed back to her and circled her feet before squeezing back inside. Jen rubbed her arms and stepped back into the warmth of the apartment. January wasn't leaving without a final reminder that it was supposed to be winter.

She turned, her gaze landing on the cheery flowers David had brought. She smiled. A gentle warmth oozed into her heart. Special and amazing. Maybe it was true.

14

David checked his watch. It was already well after seven. The office was practically deserted, and yet, here he sat, going over the proposal one final time before turning it in. It was due by nine tonight, but he wanted to get it done before the final hour. Too often the computer got overloaded at the deadline and the systems would go down, leaving people who waited to the last minute completely out of luck.

The weekend had taken a turn for the worse. He'd spent all of Saturday and most of Sunday afternoon working on the proposal. He'd texted off and on each day with Jen, but hadn't even been able to stay for lunch with everyone after the service. The start of the week hadn't been much better. He'd barely had time for a granola bar at his desk on Monday and Tuesday. Today he had run across to Mia's, but half of his sandwich was now congealing in his trash can, having sat for so long before he had a chance to get to it that it was basically inedible. He'd texted Jen a few times, a quote he'd run across over the weekend doing research, a silly story about one of the subcontractors and their inability to string sentences together coherently, but it wasn't enough. He ached to see her.

Good enough. They'd either get the project or not—and he was banking on the side of winning—they had a good proposal team, difficulties writing notwithstanding. He uploaded the document to the submission portal, double-checked all the fields were filled in, and hit send. He forwarded the email confirmation to Kurt and logged out of his machine. Seven forty-five.

It wasn't *that* late.

Would she have gone to church on a Wednesday night? There were small groups and Bible studies, but it wasn't as if they were in the age group for youth activities. And the singles didn't do anything together during the week, usually. At least, not anything spiritual. He'd overheard a handful of people in the Sunday school class talking about various happy hours. He didn't necessarily object to a drink now and then, even if it wasn't something he enjoyed personally, but to go to a bar as a church outing crossed a few lines, in his mind.

He could text. Or he could just show up. At least then he'd get to see her for a few minutes at the door. Even if she told him to go away. Resolute, David headed down to his car. He'd pick up ice cream on the way. Surely she wouldn't turn him away if he came bearing gifts.

The one benefit of leaving work so late was lighter traffic. Not that the roads were deserted. Did that ever happen around metro DC? Probably not. But still, being able to hit the speed limit— and maybe a tad above—was a bonus. He found a parking spot near her door and grabbed the tub of ice cream. His stomach flipped. David sent up a quick prayer that he wasn't moving too fast and headed for the door. Before he could talk himself out of it, he hit the doorbell.

Seconds ticked by, the ice cream freezing his hand. At least it wouldn't melt. February had started out with temperatures that plunged down to freezing at night. Though they were saying it could get up to the mid-sixties next week. After a chance of snow on Saturday. He smiled. The weather in this area was never boring.

Should he ring the bell again? Knock? Call? Maybe she wasn't home after all. One more try. He rapped on the door. This time, a faint yip reached him. Her dog was home at least.

The door opened a crack, then widened. "David? Hi."

"I got the proposal submitted and realized it was worth celebrating. Then I thought of you. I brought ice cream."

She smiled. "What flavor?"

"I wasn't sure what you liked, but my sisters say chocolate is never wrong, so I got chocolate with a fudge ribbon." He held out the tub.

Jen opened the door wider and took the ice cream. "Come on in. So you got the proposal done?"

David nodded, shutting the door behind him. He looked around her apartment. It was tidy, done in neutrals with a few splashes of color popping out on one chair, some pictures, and a pillow. Her dog was curled on the couch, watching him intently. The TV was on, a police drama paused with one of the actors mid-speech. "I—I guess I should say we, though the help from my 'team' was negligible—did. Submitted and everything. It's a pretty good bid, I think. Now we just wait and see."

"Let's sit in the kitchen. As you can see, there's a huge puzzle on my dining table. I don't know what my parents were thinking."

David followed her gesture and his eyes widened. "That's...a seriously big puzzle. But you've got all the edges done, so that's progress, right?"

"Yeah. I...have a knack, I guess." Jen shrugged. "Kitchen?"

David set down the puzzle piece he was looking at and tucked his hands in his pockets as he followed her.

Jen took two bowls out of her cupboard and set them on the counter before rooting around in a drawer. She emerged with an ice cream scoop. "How much?"

"Couple of scoops? Don't be skimpy." David flashed a grin and pulled a chair out from the tiny table that was jammed into the corner of the small space. An enormous potted plant took up most of the surface. "So, hanging out with the TV and a puzzle...is that a typical weeknight for you?"

"Yeah, probably. Sometimes I get unexpected visitors." She smiled and brought the bowls of ice cream over. "Usually it's my mom, Rebecca, or Sara though. And they don't usually bring ice cream."

"Well, that's something, then. It's a pretty good way to spend an evening. I'll be glad when I can stop bringing work home and actually watch a show instead of having it on for background noise and missing most of it. That episode you're watching? I think I got about five minutes of it." He dipped his spoon into the dessert. She'd barely put any into her bowl. Should he mention it? "Was this not a good flavor?"

Jen paused with her spoon nearly to her mouth. "No, it's great. Why?"

"I...you're not hungry?"

She sighed and put the spoon down. "I don't have a metabolism that lets me eat whatever I want, whenever I want."

"You're beautiful."

Jen flushed and glanced down at her bowl. "Thanks. Anyway. You like the show?"

He nodded. Better to drop it. But did she really not understand how lovely she was? "One of my favorites. Have you been watching since it started?"

"Yeah—even suffered through that half-season where they tried to replace the female lead with that big-chested bimbo."

He laughed. "That was hard to get through. I was glad when they finally killed her off, even if they did go for the sap and leave the lead with a broken heart. Whatever, man, rub some dirt on it and do your job."

"Oh, it's that easy? What if she was the love of his life? I like the new dimension it added to his character."

David scoffed. "No one as dumb as she was would ever be the love of his life. He's too brainy for that. He was the ultimate— brainy and hardcore—now he's such a cry baby, I half expect him to start weeping in the middle of a foot chase."

"He's not that bad."

"Finish the episode you're watching and then tell me that." David scooped up another bite. "What else do you watch?"

"I like some of the competition-based reality shows. Cooking, singing, doesn't matter. As long as there's a decent prize at the end and the people are looking to kick start an actual career. Not the ones where they're just looking for fifteen minutes of fame for being on TV."

He laughed. "I'll deny it if you ever tell anyone, but I like those too. Ever try out the recipes?"

"From the shows?" Jen poked at the ice cream in her bowl then licked her spoon.

"Yeah. They're usually up on the website a day or two after the episode airs. Some have been pretty good."

"You cook."

His eyebrows lifted. She sounded stunned. Bordering on amazed. "Not as often as I'd like, but I've been known to."

She shook her head. "No way."

"Are you saying I'm lying?"

Her eyes darted to one side and she pulled her lower lip between her teeth. "Well..."

"Challenge accepted. Busy Saturday?"

She blinked. "Um. No?"

"Now you are. Anything you don't eat?"

"I don't particularly care for shellfish. It's not an allergy, really, but..." Jen scrunched her nose.

"No shellfish. Check. Can I pick you up at five?"

She tapped her spoon against the bowl. "You're cooking. Why don't I just drive myself? That way you don't have to try and plan around a break to come get me."

"You're sure?"

She nodded.

His parents would be appalled. On the other hand, he didn't make a habit of cooking for his dates. He'd never even cooked for Soo-Yi. It had never seemed right. This did. Being around Jen was like being at home. Comfortable. But not in a boring or forgettable way. If anything, being around her had him more aware of...everything. "Okay. Five still work?"

"I can do that. I'll need your address."

David slipped his phone out of his pocket and tapped his address into a text message. "There."

Things were silent for several heartbeats. Should he...what? He didn't want to talk about work, especially since she hadn't brought it up. "Want some help with your puzzle?"

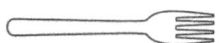

"You're cooking for her?" Ji shook hot sauce on her chicken wings. "You've only cooked for the family once. She really is special."

David nodded. "She is. I don't think she realizes it though."

"I've been thinking about that. I wonder if the problem is less a self-esteem issue and more depression."

Depression? He pursed his lips. Maybe. "The two probably feed each other, don't they?"

"You catch on fast."

He smiled and took a bite of his own chicken. Ji had gone through some fairly serious depression after she and Jared broke up. It had been a rough time for the family. Their church didn't believe Christians could be depressed. Though they never had any issues with physical illness, mental illness fell solely into the camp of spiritual warfare. Not that it wasn't—the devil had a grand time convincing Christians they were worthless. It got them to do his work for him. But as his family—and ultimately his church—had learned while walking alongside Ji, mental illnesses shouldn't be a cause for shame and ostracism.

"Anyway, the more I thought about it, the more that seemed like something I should mention. You maybe don't remember..."

"I remember." David touched his sister's hand. "I was young, but not that young. And it was a rough time."

Ji nodded and looked away. "I had trouble after both kids were born, too. I think maybe there's a predisposition in me."

"Why didn't you say something?"

She shrugged. "I'd beaten it once, you know? I thought surely it wasn't something I'd have to deal with again. But it was—is. If I'm honest, I fight it every day. Min is a rock, so supportive. But I know it's not easy to love me. You need to know that, going in. Loving someone who battles depression is hard."

Loving? It made him catch his breath. And yet... "I appreciate that. I think it's what I'm supposed to do."

Ji smiled. "She's lucky to have you."

"She just doesn't realize it yet."

Chuckling, Ji took a long pull from her soda. "Why do you say that?"

"She keeps putting up walls, pushing back ever so slightly."

"That's not surprising, if I'm right."

David nodded. It did put a new spin on things. Maybe she wasn't disinterested. "So keep trying?"

"Unless she unequivocally tells you to stop. There is an element of 'no means no' to be kept in mind."

"How do I know?"

"Pray. A lot. I will too."

He sighed. Why couldn't God send down a daily to-do list? Or even weekly? Of course, if He did, there'd be no need to pray and trust. Which probably answered the question. "Thanks, Ji."

15

Butterflies danced in her stomach. What had she been thinking when she agreed to this? Dinner at his apartment? If that didn't say "date," nothing did. And they weren't dating. They weren't suited to that. Hadn't they agreed on that?

Rebecca and Sara hadn't been any help last night, either. They thought it was cute. And okay, maybe it was. But...how could anything come out of it? Rebecca had gone on for what seemed like forever about how she needed to let their bad date go. Sure, maybe she did. It was never good to drag that around. Except she couldn't. Just like all the bad things people said to her, her bad experiences followed her around, replaying in her head whenever doubt opened the door. And doubt was never far away.

Why couldn't she be like normal people and shrug it off? Why couldn't she, even in the middle of hanging out with friends and having fun, accept that the people she was with really liked her and wanted to be with her? Instead, she spent half the time questioning why they were bothering, wondering what they were after and when they were going to realize they could do so much better and walk away. Why did it take so much energy to get herself out the door and then even more to stay? And by the time she got home, the doubts and fears were so all-consuming she only wanted to pull the covers up over her head and sleep for the next three days.

But somehow, life kept marching on. Which meant she had to as well.

A year ago, the anti-depressants she finally broke down and got from her doctor were enough to make it less of a struggle. And even though Doctor Mancini had been a jerk, some of the coping techniques she'd learned in therapy had started to help. Why didn't they still do the job? Why couldn't faith be enough? Jen sighed. Maybe her mom was right. Maybe she did need to go back to the doctor and see about increasing her medication. More therapy? She wasn't there yet. Although...at some point, didn't you have to admit your failure?

Focus on the positive. For whatever reason, whether or not it made sense, David continued to act interested. It was worth the effort to meet him half way. Because she couldn't lie to herself anymore. She liked him. And no amount of praying was changing that. If anything, the more she prayed, the more David seemed to pursue.

So. She was going to get out of the car, go into his building, and have dinner. Jen took a deep breath and pushed open her car door. His building was fancy. One of the newer high rise building on the edges of Tyson's. Rent must be insane. Of course, he was several levels above her salary-wise, so it probably was no big deal, but...what would it be like to live in something all shiny and new with glass and chrome everywhere? She wrinkled her nose. Her complex was older and all brick. But they'd replaced the carpet fairly recently and her neighbors were friendly. Plus, no one minded Tribble. That was definitely a bonus. Could you even have a dog in a place like this?

With a nod to the security guard in the entrance, Jen made her way to the elevators and pressed the button. Her complex was all walk-up. Yet another reason to have the ground level, even if the grassy spot for Tribble hadn't pushed her over the edge. The car arrived and she stepped in, pressing David's floor. The ride up was smooth and fast. Before she was ready, she was standing in front of his apartment door, reminding herself to breathe.

"Right on time." David grinned as he held open the door. "Have any trouble finding it?"

She shook her head and looked around his living room. It was clean and almost meticulously organized. Books were shelved neatly, there wasn't even a speck of dust on the glass-topped coffee table, and his black leather sofa gleamed in the soft light from the lamps on the end tables on either side. "This is nice. Have you lived here long?"

"Since they built the place five years ago. My older brother works for the investment company that owns it, he got me on the list before it was open to the public. That's how I snagged one of the corners, with two balconies. They went fast."

"I bet." She tucked her hands in her pockets. "I should have offered to bring something. I'm sorry. It didn't occur to me."

"It's not a problem. Can I get you something to drink? I have iced tea, various sodas, water?"

"Water is fine. It smells good."

He chuckled. "You sound surprised."

"No."

He eyed her, eyebrows raised.

"Okay, maybe a little." Of course, it could be takeout. Even if it was, it was a nice gesture. But it didn't smell like takeout.

"Why don't you have a seat, I'll get you some water and bring out the first course." David gestured to the two-person table set against the floor-to-ceiling window. A single bright-yellow daisy stood in a bud vase in the center, between two place settings of simple white china on black placemats. David pulled out a chair.

Jen sat, running her finger over the edge of the placemat. Silk? Couldn't be. Who would use silk placemats? What if something dripped on them?

David winked and strode away, disappearing through a doorway that must be the kitchen. Jen looked out the window at the cars making their way toward the mall, maybe to shop or see a movie, typical Saturday night things. Dusk was already falling. Lights were coming on. From up here, it almost looked peaceful.

"It's a great view. I get distracted by it, sometimes, when I'm supposed to be working."

Jen jumped, her heart racing, and not all from surprise. Just his proximity was enough to send her pulse into overdrive. "I can imagine." She accepted the water and took a long drink. "Thanks."

David set a plate holding two stuffed portabella mushrooms in the center of the table before sitting across from her and stretching out his hand. "Can we pray?"

"Of course." Jen wrapped her fingers around his—how could something be electrifying and comforting at the same time?—and bowed her head.

"Dear Jesus, thank you for Jen. Thank you for making her the amazing woman that she is and for bringing her into my life. Bless our time together. Let words we say and the things we think bring you honor and glory. Thank you for the meal we're about to eat, bless it to our bodies. Amen." He squeezed her hand before letting go.

One corner of Jen's mouth curved up. His prayer had eased something inside her. It was unconventional—at least in her mind. Who prayed like that for the person they were sitting with? And yet, it had made her feel special. Cherished. She'd analyze it later. "Those look amazing."

Using two forks as makeshift tongs, he lifted one mushroom and placed it on her plate, then repeated the action for his own. "Thanks. Did you see the season where there were two cowboys competing?"

"Mmm. I think so. There was the girl from Alaska on that one, too, right?"

David chuckled. "That's the one. These mushrooms were on one of the episodes, though I forget which one. I've always liked portabellas though, so I knew I had to try them. They never posted the recipe, but I've played around a little and this is the most successful result."

Flavors exploded in her mouth as she took a bite. "You came up with this on your own? No recipe?"

He shrugged. "I re-watched it a few times, listening to what they said they were doing and taking notes. You like it?"

"A lot. You have a recipe?"

"I do. And, given the right incentive, I might share it with you."

Incentive? Given the sparkle in his eyes, he was teasing. But still. "Yeah? What'd you have in mind?"

"Hold that thought. I think our main course just buzzed." David stood and disappeared back into the kitchen. Accompanied by the rustling and banging in the kitchen, Jen finished her mushroom. It really was very good. Before long, he returned with two plates of food. "Here we go. Chicken Cordon Blue with asparagus and a parsnip puree."

"Fancy." Jen leaned closer and sniffed the artfully decorated blob of what appeared to be slightly runnier than usual mashed potatoes. "I don't know that I've ever had a parsnip before. What is it?"

"It looks like a white carrot, but the taste is sharp and, I don't know, tangy? Try it. If you don't like it, you don't have to eat it. There's no clean plate club here, I promise."

Jen chuckled. "Good to know. Do you cook this fancy for all your friends?"

"I...really only cook for my family. And even then, not often. Special occasions, you know?"

He didn't do this all the time? That made this something special. A date. She'd already figured it was a date, but not a capital D date. She looked down at the food, her mouth watering. She dipped the tines of her fork into the parsnips and tasted them. "Huh. Not what I was expecting. But good."

He grinned and started cutting into his chicken. "I'm glad you like it."

"You really don't do this for everyone?"

He shook his head.

"Well, thanks."

"Any time. I mean it." He held her gaze. "I'd like to make this a habit."

Heat crawled across her cheeks. "Why?"

David set his knife and fork down, a frown etched into his features. "Why do you say that?"

Jen drew her eyebrows together. "Say what?"

"When I say something about wanting to spend time with you, or how much I like you, you ask why."

She winced. She said it aloud. "I thought I kept that internal. Sorry."

"Even if you didn't say it, you thought it. So my question stands. Why?"

She shrugged. How could she explain it? "I don't expect you to understand."

"Try? I'd really like to know."

Her appetite evaporated and she nudged her plate away, crossing her arms on the table. "I guess I don't understand why anyone would think I matter. I'm just me. I'm not a particularly amazing programmer, or team lead, or, well, anything. I'm average. I don't have a marvelous figure, I'm not beautiful. There's nothing about me that's special."

David reached across the table and pried one of her hands loose, clasping it in his own. "I promise you, none of that is the truth. You wouldn't be a team lead—or even still on the team as a programmer—if you weren't good at it. I know Jenisse. She runs a tight ship and doesn't suffer fools gladly. For her to put you in a team lead position on any project, let alone one with customer contact? It means she thinks very highly of you. And she's a good judge of character and ability. The rest? So much of that is in the eye of the beholder and this beholder, these eyes? They say you're wrong."

Jen looked away, turning to stare out the window. Headlights glowed like diamonds on the road below, their edges blurring as her eyes filled will tears. She blinked rapidly. The last thing she wanted to do was ruin the night by crying.

His fingers tightened on hers. "So when I say I want to spend time with you? It's because I think you're beautiful, intelligent, interesting, and fun to be around. And I wish there was a way to convince you to believe me."

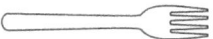

Jen stared up at the ceiling. Tribble was snoring at her feet, but that wasn't what kept her awake. David's words echoed in her mind. Would they be loud enough to erase the other words from so many different people that said the opposite? Her head knew he probably right. Her heart was a different matter. Though they'd always insisted otherwise, she knew her parents regretted not having more children. She wasn't enough for them. Would she be if she was different somehow? Or was it a simple matter of quantity?

She sighed. Her parents loved her. That wasn't a question. And her team at work liked, maybe even respected, her.

So why couldn't she accept that? Believe it? Why did the doubts creep in, crippling her?

David said he liked her. He'd said more than that, but it boiled down to the same thing. And if someone like him could say it, and mean it...maybe it was time she figured out how to believe it.

Jen fidgeted with her purse as she waited. The church secretary periodically looked up from whatever it was she was typing and smiled, but otherwise seemed content not to make conversation. Not that Jen wanted to make conversation. She wasn't one hundred percent sure she even wanted to be here. She ran her hand over the upholstery of the chair. How could something look so comfortable and yet fail on every point? It was the scratchiest, hardest chair she'd ever sat in. Maybe it kept people from coming and hanging out in the office. But who'd do that?

Pastor Paul Brown's office door opened and he poked his head out. His gaze landed on her. "Jennifer? Sorry to keep you waiting, come on in."

She took a deep breath and stood, willing her heart to quit racing. This was just the pastor. He always seemed friendly. Hopefully that would prove to be the case. She managed a weak smile. "No problem. Thanks for seeing me."

Paul closed the door and gestured to the two chairs arranged conversationally in the corner of his office. "Have a seat and tell me what's on your mind."

Jen eyed the chairs as she sat. They looked the same as the ones in the waiting area. Well, at least it would keep the meeting short. She swallowed and wound her fingers together to keep them still. "I'm not sure how to start. I..." She paused and searched for words. Better, probably, to just spit it out. "I struggle with depression."

Paul nodded. "So many people do. Are you on medication?"

"Yes. But lately it hasn't been helping like it used to and...is it because I'm lacking somehow? In faith?"

"No." Paul leaned forward, his expression earnest. "Depression isn't an indicator for a lack of faith any more than another disease is. But for whatever reason, Satan is really good at convincing Christians that depression is purely a spiritual problem. I'm not saying there can't be a spiritual component to it—obviously that's true of any circumstance. But we have to, at some point, fall back on God's sovereignty, and ask Him to use us and our particular situation for His glory."

Use depression for His glory? "How would that even happen?"

Paul chuckled. "That's a big question that I'm not sure I can answer. But if depression draws you closer to Christ, then that's certainly going to be one way. Beyond that? You never know who's going to see you walk through something and be impacted by it."

Jen nodded. That made sense. Sort of. "So...I'm not a failure as a Christian for needing medication? For probably needing to get my doctor to increase my dose?"

"No."

That's it? A simple no? Where was the lecture about how maybe she should wait and trust God to get her through? Or to pray harder for healing? She smiled, her eyes filling with tears. "Thank you."

"Anytime. Can we pray?"

Jen bowed her head and let the pastor's words wash over her. They brought a peace that had been missing—though she hadn't realized it until it was back. A tear slipped down her cheek. She'd call her doctor on her way in to work. And then she'd call David and see if she could pick up lunch. She was running late, which she'd expected and was why she'd left Tribble at her parent's house for the day, but some things—some people—were worth making the time for. David was one of them.

16

David hid his phone under the conference table and checked his messages. The ten-minute meeting was heading into its second hour. At this rate, he wasn't going to be out before his one o'clock meeting started. Forget having the time to try and convince Jen to go grab lunch with him. Even running across the street to Mia's was looking iffy at this point.

While the presenter droned on, he tapped out a few quick replies to emails then opened his texts. Jen. He smiled. This was the first time she'd sought him out. Maybe their conversation on Saturday had gotten through. He checked the time. Maybe he *could* squeeze food in, especially since she was bringing it with her. He tapped back a reply and shot up a quick prayer that the meeting would be over by the time he told her. The last thing he wanted to do was stand her up. Talk about undoing all the work you'd put into something.

"Did you have anything to add, David?"

He started and looked up. "No. I think you covered it."

One of his colleagues snickered but Kurt nodded as his cell phone began to ring. "Great, then I think we're set. That'll be all."

"Nice recovery." Martin elbowed David in the ribs as he brushed past.

"Thanks." David collected his laptop and coffee mug and aimed for the door before Kurt could think of something to add to his workload. Thankfully, Kurt's phone call had engrossed the man in the conversation. Lunch with Jen was looking more and more possible.

Back in his office, David hooked his laptop back up to the monitor and scrolled through the email that had accumulated over the last twenty minutes. Why did people send so much email? Was it impossible to just get up, walk down the hall, and ask someone? Most of the questions had been answered. So that was good. But he needed to get the team lead position filled. Fast. The applicant he'd thought was going to be the internal transfer he needed had backed out at the last minute. And now, Stephen was gone, so handoff wasn't going to happen. Whoever they brought in was going to get dumped in the deep end and forced to swim. Which wasn't a bad way to test their mettle, even if it was going to be rocky for the first couple of weeks. Now they just needed someone to take the job. He needed to check in with Min, see if he was serious about changing jobs. The brief conversation he'd had with Kurt about the possibility of hiring his brother-in-law had gone well, so if Min wanted the job, David could basically guarantee it was his.

He tapped out an email to Min and another to his contact in HR.

"Hey. You ready to eat?" Jen stood in his doorway, a plastic bag in her hand and two big drinks hugged close by her other arm.

David checked the time and hit send. "Absolutely. Would you mind eating here? I have a one o'clock that I can't miss."

"Sure."

David crossed to the round table by his whiteboards. He pushed a pile of proposal research and status reports out of the way and pulled out one of the four chairs before reaching for the drinks. "Here. Let me help."

Once he'd taken the drinks, Jen shook her arm and set the bag on the table. "Those are cold. I got sandwiches, hope that's okay?"

"Sounds great." David waited for her to sit before doing so himself. He wanted to ask what prompted the lunch, but he didn't want to make it weird. He cleared his throat. "You're just getting in?"

"Yeah, well, about thirty minutes ago, but yeah. I stopped at the church to see Pastor Brown." Jen glanced over her shoulder then got up and shut the door to his office before returning to her seat.

David's eyebrows lifted. "Everything okay?"

"Sort of. I take anti-depressants, and lately they don't seem to be doing such a great job. It took my mom, and you, pointing it out for me to realize how bad it was getting. Again."

David nodded. So his sister had been right. She always had been smart.

Jen narrowed her eyes. "You're not surprised."

"My sister struggles with depression. Has for a long time. She pointed out to me that there were some similarities."

"Was that before Saturday, or after?"

"Before."

Jen was silent for several long seconds. David looked down at his sandwich and began to unwrap it. Should he not have told her? He wasn't going to lie though. She took a deep breath. "Knowing that, or I guess suspecting it, you still said that you wanted to know me better? To spend time with me?"

He put the sandwich down and cocked his head to the side. "Why wouldn't I?"

Jen blinked rapidly. "Because no one's ever chosen me like that. Warts and all. Usually it sends people—guys—running."

"Then they're idiots."

She laughed. The sound was strained and watery, but there was still a hint of humor in it. "Okay. Then...if you're not an idiot, does that mean we're dating? Like a couple? Exclusive?"

He couldn't stop the grin as he reached over to take one of her hands, as much to stop the nervous twisting of her fingers as to sate the desire to touch her. "I'd like that, if you would."

She nodded.

"Then that's that." He brought her fingers to his lips and, holding her gaze, kissed them. Sparks flew between them. David longed for the taste of her lips, but his office was the wrong place for that. "The Pastor helped you with that?"

Jen giggled, an almost desperate sound, and tugged her hand free. As she unwrapped her own sandwich, she broke eye-contact. "No. I wanted to know if it was me, something wrong with me. Obviously it's something wrong with me, but my faith?"

David's heart ached for her. Ji had struggled with the same questions. He remembered listening to her sob while her parents and the elders from the church met with her in the living room after he was supposed to be in bed. At the time, they'd been convinced that there was, in fact, something wrong with her spiritually. "And?"

"He said it's no different than any other illness. That God can heal me, but He might not. And that what's important is that I trust and seek Him and get the help I need."

David breathed a silent prayer of thanks for this pastor who he barely knew. It made him appreciate the church even more than he already did. "That's good."

She nodded and cleared her throat. "You should probably eat if you're going to be on time to your meeting."

He glanced at the time on his phone and nodded. "One quick thing, if I can backtrack a little?"

"Yeah?"

"Since you're my girlfriend now, will you come to a wedding with me this weekend for Valentine's Day?"

My girlfriend. The words had echoed in his head all afternoon. Could they be any more middle school? She'd said yes without batting an eye, but she must think he was an idiot. Girlfriend. He shook his head and texted Colin that he did, in fact, have a plus one coming after all. Hopefully it wasn't too late. Knowing Colin, he'd make it work.

He frowned at his phone. Girlfriend. That meant he should text her—or call—right? Not that he had anything to say. His afternoon had been a fairly typical one and she couldn't possibly be interested in hearing about it. He snickered as his phone began to ring, Jen's face filling the screen. Maybe she was interested after all.

"I was just thinking about you." David settled back against the arm of the couch and stretched his legs out, his sock-clad feet crossed at the ankle.

There was a smile in her voice. "That's handy. Good things, I hope?"

"Always." Maybe that was a tiny lie. He'd certainly had his share of doubts and questions, and he wasn't ruling out the possibility of their return. But that was what happened in a relationship, wasn't it? And when it did, you worked through it, prayed through it, and focused on the positive.

"This wedding. Any idea how formal it is? I'm trying to decide if I need to squeeze a shopping trip in, or if I can wear something I already have."

"Colin told me to just wear a dark suit, with a tie."

"And you're in the wedding, right?"

"Yep."

"Hmm. Then I'm probably fine. Which is good, because I'd rather face a firing squad than go shopping."

David laughed.

"I'm serious. Rebecca and Sara dragged me shopping a couple of weeks ago, and while it was fun, I'm not in a hurry to repeat the experience. What if...do you think I could wear the dress I wore to Ben and Rebecca's wedding? Or is that too much?"

A slow smile curved his lips and his mouth went dry. She looked amazing in that dress. "I'm sure that would be perfect."

"Not too much? You're sure?"

"If it's up to me, I'm sure. You're—that dress is—I mean..." David stopped and huffed out a breath. "You'll be the most beautiful woman there."

"I'm...not sure how to respond to that."

He winced. What had Ji said about taking it slow and giving Jen time to realize he was serious? It'd take time for Jen to get past the self-hatred that depression can cause. He needed to remember that. "That's okay." Time to change the subject. "How was the rest of your day?"

"This is getting to be a habit. What brings you here tonight?" Jackson tucked a bookmark into the thick tome he was reading and set it aside.

David shrugged and slid into the booth opposite his friend. "Nothing else sounded interesting. Some of the gang from work was headed downtown. I guess there's a big pub crawl going on for Valentine's weekend. Jen said Rebecca and Sara had made plans with Amy? So I figured I'd see if you were here. And you are. No Ben?"

Jackson chuckled. "He and Zach are probably going to show up. Paige is actually out with the girls. She put her second-in-command in charge tonight. He said we can order off the menu if we want to eat."

David laughed. "That seems fair. Especially if he's not used to running the kitchen on a Friday night. Do we have a menu?"

"Supposedly one of the servers will be by. I wasn't in a hurry. Hungry?"

"If Ben and Zach are coming, we can wait. Or at least I can. How's the wedding prep going? You're getting closer by the day."

"By definition." Jackson's smile took the sting out of his words. "I think we're set. I have plane tickets and hotel reservations for the honeymoon, my tux is rented, and our rings will be ready to pick up next week. Beyond that, I just have to show up, right?"

"Don't look at me. Sounds good though. Maybe you should double check with Paige?"

"Probably should. Though, all things considered, she's been pretty low key about the whole thing. I was expecting more drama. But then, Paige isn't one for drama to begin with." Jackson shifted and frowned over at the expediting shelf where servers picked up food and carried it to the diners. "Maybe I should go grab us some menus. Or at least let someone know we could use some water."

"David? Hey, man." Zach slid into the booth next to him with a grin. Ben took the seat next to Jackson. "I come bearing menus and a promise that someone will be right with us."

"Guess that answers that." Jackson reached for the leather folder. "Do you know, I don't think I've ordered off the menu more than twice?"

"That's two times more than me." David chuckled and flipped the second menu open, angling it so Zach could also see. "What's good?"

"Everything. Paige doesn't put up with food that doesn't taste good. Plus, she changes the menu seasonally, so I doubt very much having eaten here before will be any help in choosing what to order." Jackson shrugged. "That said, you really can't go wrong."

"I can attest to that, having actually ordered off the menu a few times." Ben craned his neck to see the menu that Jackson was holding. "So, Zach, you said you needed to talk to us. What's up?"

David grimaced. "Is this a former-roommate thing? I can go."

"Don't be silly. You're part of the group, especially now that you and Jen are officially dating."

"What? When did that happen? Congrats, man." Ben reached across the table to punch David's shoulder. "And how did you find that out before me?"

"Not being married, I still listen when Amy talks instead of just giving a default 'yes, Dear' when there's silence?"

Jackson and David laughed while Ben sputtered. "I listen just fine, thank you very much."

"Mmhmm. Which is how I know something that Amy only knows because Rebecca told her. Got it." Zach nodded, his expression facetious.

"Whatever. You were saying, Zach?" Ben crossed his arms.

David hunched his shoulders. "I really don't mind."

Zach elbowed his ribs. "Stop. You're fine. Here's the thing—"

A server appeared at their table with water glasses and a pitcher. "Hi, sorry, we're slammed tonight, but I promised Paige I'd keep you happy. What can I get you?"

Zach visibly relaxed as they went around the table and ordered. What was the problem? David drummed his fingers on his leg. From Zach's body language it was serious. Should he offer to leave again? No, twice was enough. They were straightforward enough that they would've said yes if they'd really wanted him to go.

The server disappeared and Zach drew in a deep breath. "Like I was saying, when I moved downtown, I'm not sure I completely thought it through."

Ben frowned. "What do you mean? Are you and Amy having trouble?"

"Not like that, no. But I didn't think about what it would be like to live so close to her. We share a wall, for crying out loud. I'm tempted to call her dad and have him put a lock on the outside of my apartment door, so she can lock me in after we say goodnight. Except...I'm not completely convinced she would." Zach dipped his head and reached up to massage his neck. "Amy wants this big Christmas wedding. It's her dream. I guess I'm fine with that, provided we stay within a rational budget. Her parents seem pretty reasonable about what they'll allow her to spend on it. But I don't know how we're going to last that long when we're already practically living together."

Ben reached for his water. "That's tough. I'm not going to be any help, you know that's one of the reasons we decided to elope. I'll admit it also got us out of the three-ring circus Becca's mom was trying to plan, but I don't know what we would've done if Bec had wanted the circus."

"Paige has always only wanted a small wedding. We were only holding off on setting a date because we hadn't known each other as long as some couples. Honestly, the two of you have been friends for so long, and then dated...a long engagement doesn't make much sense."

Zach scoffed. "Try telling Amy that. You have any advice, David?"

"Me? I just started dating someone for the first time in a long time. I'm not sure I could even offer dating advice at this point." David frowned. "Although, I do have sisters. One went for the huge American wedding extravaganza and the other did a smaller, more traditional wedding, which at our church means it was part of the Sunday service and then a whole bunch of food afterward."

Zach leaned forward. "And?"

David shrugged. "They both ended up with the same result: a marriage."

Jackson and Ben chuckled.

"No, don't laugh. That's potentially helpful." Zach leaned back as the server brought plates over and put them on the table. "Maybe I need to remind her of what our end goal is."

"What's that?" David unrolled the napkin holding his silverware and laid it in his lap.

"A marriage that starts out on the right foot because we've been true to Jesus and His calling throughout our courtship." Zach pulled his glass closer, but didn't take a sip.

Jackson aimed his fork at Zach. "Can't you have that *and* a big wedding?"

Zach shook his head. "Not if I'm still living in her building from now until Christmas. It's only been two months—not even two full months—and we've almost messed up three times. Ten more months is just asking for trouble."

17

"This was the best idea." Amy scooted down so the bubbles of the hot tub covered her shoulders. "How did I not know your town house community had a hot tub and that you could reserve it?"

Rebecca grinned. "I didn't even know. Ben is, apparently, one of those people who read the manuals. So when he moved in, he read through all the various home owner-y things I had laying around, including the home owner's association book. Two phone calls later, I had a reservation for tonight and the beginnings of a girl's night idea."

"Yay for Ben." Jen flicked water at Rebecca. "But boo on you. You've lived here how long? Sara and I could've been relaxing in splendor if you took the time to read."

"Ooh, good point. Uncool, Rebecca. Very uncool. Didn't you have to sign something saying you agreed to the HOA regs when you bought the house?" Sarah laid her head back and stretched her legs out.

Rebecca shrugged. "Yeah, but the realtor gave me the high points and I figured if I needed to know anything, I could look it up then. And yes, now I realize that was short sighted. I'm sorry."

"You're forgiven. This time." Jen crossed her arms over her midsection under the water. It was ridiculous to worry about what she looked like in her bathing suit when the only people here were her friends. Female friends, at that. And yet she still wished for a giant t-shirt to hide in. At least the rapidly bubbling water was hard to see through. "How's the wedding planning going?"

"Mine's done." Rebecca grinned. "And can I just say thank you, Jesus, for that. I don't know how the two of you are able to stand making decision after decision after decision without wanting to chuck it all and elope."

Paige rolled her eyes. "It's not that bad. We're set. At this point we have a few weeks of breathing room before we have to start picking things up the week of the big day."

"It'll be here before you know it. I can't wait." Rebecca wiggled in her seat. "The bridesmaid dresses you chose are gorgeous."

Amy wrinkled her nose. "I haven't done much with ours yet. Christmas seems so far off, there's plenty of time."

"I'm not sure that's true. I read some blog posts this week about venues booking up eighteen months in advance."

Jen frowned at Sara. "Why are you reading wedding blogs?"

Sara lifted a shoulder. "Things are going really well with Luc. It never hurts to have an eye on the industry, right?"

Jen clamped her lips together. She wasn't going to launch into a lecture about how her friend barely knew the guy. Even if they'd been together nearly two months now, he was rarely in town. Long distance dating didn't give you a chance to discover flaws.

Amy sighed. "Yeah, I guess."

"What's wrong? It seems to me you should be more excited about marrying the man of your dreams." Rebecca leaned toward Amy, her gaze intent. "Are you two having problems?"

"No. Not really."

Jen arched a brow. "That sounds like 'kind of.'"

Amy looked away and took several deep breaths.

"Hey, what's going on? Maybe we can help?" Rebecca reached over and rubbed Amy's shoulder.

"It's really hard now that he lives next door. We walk to and from school together, eat dinner at one of our apartments and...there's no one who'd know, you know, if maybe he didn't go back across the hall. Or I didn't." Amy's tongue darted between her lips. "And nothing's happened, but it gets harder to do the right thing every time. You must think I'm horrible."

"I don't see what the big deal is. You're engaged and it's just sex. Why not move in together and be done with the craziness?" Sara reached behind her for the bottle of water she'd stashed there when they'd first climbed into the hot tub.

Jen's mouth dropped open. She and Sara had had this conversation before, but to be so frank about it? In front of everyone? "Sara. She and Zach are trying to do the right thing."

"Whatever. It's not 'the right thing'." Sara made air quotes. "It's an antiquated and unrealistic expectation that has no place in today's world. Seriously, how old were people when they got married in the Bible? Twelve? Thirteen? Anyone can be abstinent that long. And it's not like you're out sleeping with every guy you see. You're engaged, for crying out loud. That's close enough to married to count."

For several minutes, the only sound was the bubbling of the jets.

Paige cleared her throat. "So, you're not planning to wait until you're married?"

"Pfft. That ship sailed a long time ago. And it's no big deal, as long as you love the guy and he loves you. My personal rule is that there's no one else at the same time, but as long as everyone's on the same page..." Sara shrugged.

"Seriously?" Jen's stomach twisted. She'd known Sara wasn't committed to abstinence, but to be so casual about it? She'd been sure her friend would, at a minimum, hold out for being engaged. "So...you and Luc?"

Sara nodded. "Yeah, last weekend. It's been over a month. Guys expect it. You realize that, don't you?"

"Jackson doesn't."

"Ben never did, either. Even though I know he—well, we both—struggled. It was important to us."

"Zach's in that camp, too. Honestly, he's been the stronger one of the two of us. If it was just up to me, I don't know what would've happened."

Sara shook her head. "I don't understand you people. I already know Jen's ready to die a shriveled old maid if someone doesn't snap her up. Why can't you see it's unrealistic? God designed our bodies for this."

"Inside marriage." Jen bristled. She couldn't keep quiet anymore. Even if she didn't have a fiancé, she'd dated and been tempted. "As a mirror of the intimacy that's supposed to exist between Christ and the church. Not something for us to toss around, willy nilly. If that makes me a shriveled old maid, then so be it. But if you're sleeping with multiple people outside of marriage, then I think we all know what word that makes you."

"You believe that if you want. Your thought process is old fashioned. Maybe it works for you. But there are a lot of Christians who understand the reality of the situation. Anyway, you were asking for advice, I gave you my opinion. What right do you have to judge me for it, anyway? Isn't that just as big a sin as sex?" Sara shrugged.

"No. Pointing out where another believer isn't following what Christ—what the Bible—says, isn't judging. Not in the way you mean, at least. It's iron sharpening iron and speaking the truth in order to try and keep sister in Christ from stumbling. I'm sorry you feel judged, but maybe that's just the Holy Spirit activating your conscience." Jen crossed her arms.

"Whatever." Sara sniffed and turned pointedly away from Jen, looking at Amy. "If you're really going to stick to something that outdated and unnecessary then you should just go ahead and get married now."

Amy frowned. "Didn't you ever dream of your wedding day? Don't you want that moment in the spotlight? The big frilly dress? The party where all eyes are on you?"

"Can't you make that happen faster?" Jen rubbed her fingers together. They were starting to wrinkle up. "Or could you do a small ceremony and then have a fancy party later?"

"I guess. Maybe...maybe Zach and I need to consider that." Amy sighed and pushed herself out of the hot tub, perching on the edge.

"It's kind of the same idea Sara had, just flipped." Jen chuckled.

Rebecca laughed. "You have a point. And I don't know about the rest of you, but I'm getting pruney. What do you say we move this party back to my house and dig out the ice cream?"

Jen pressed her hand to her stomach to quell the butterflies. These were David's friends, not people that she'd known first. Meeting new people was always an iffy proposition, but to go to their wedding? Why had she agreed to this?

David slipped his arm around her waist and leaned close. "You look beautiful. Colin and Rachel are good people, smart. They're going to love you."

His words sent tingles down her spine. Okay. She could do this. She managed a weak smile. "You look great, too. By the way."

"Thanks." David steered them toward the small chapel where the wedding was going to be. It was in the middle of a quaint, historic part of Annapolis. Jen looked around as they crossed the short walkway and up the stairs of the little church. She could see getting married somewhere like this. He pulled open the door and held it for her.

Jen stepped through and stopped. What an adorable place. A red carpet runner went up the short aisle between the wooden pews. Stained glass windows made graceful arches down each outer wall. And the pulpit...so much carved wood and an enormous rose window. It was like a little glimpse of what church in heaven must be like. "Where is everyone?"

David paused and glanced at his watch. "We're a little early, let's head down and see what we see. I know it's going to be a small wedding."

As he spoke, a man entered the church through a side door. He stopped when he saw them, then grinned. "David."

"Colin. I was just beginning to wonder if we'd gotten the wrong place." David's hand in the small of her back was warm, comforting. "This is Jen. Jen, meet the groom, Colin."

Colin made quick work of the space between them and extended his hand. "Pleasure to meet you. Thanks for coming. It'll be nice to have someone here who isn't part of the wedding."

Jen's eyebrows shot up. "I'm the only guest?"

Colin grinned at David. "I said it was small."

"Think of it this way, you'll have a great view." David's fingers tightened at her waist.

"Sure. That's...oh, we brought you a gift." She reached into her purse and withdrew an envelope. "Congratulations on your wedding."

Colin slipped the envelope into the inside pocket of his suit. "Thanks. Why don't you have a seat? Rachel's almost ready, according to her uncle, so we should be able to get things going before too much longer."

Jen fought against the heaviness that tried to suffocate her. She wasn't giving in to this, not today. Her doctor couldn't see her until next week, and even then, it wasn't as if the medication would start to work immediately. She needed better coping mechanisms. Find a blessing. That's what her mother always said, back when Jen was still trying to convince herself that feeling blue now and then wasn't as big a problem as it had already become. Blessing number one? David.

It was as if he knew she was struggling. He kept in contact with her, just a light touch. Nothing overwhelming or possessive, but a little reminder that he was here. She shot him a smile and tried to infuse it with gratitude.

A tiny crack of light wormed its way through the darkness in her mind.

Okay, blessing two? Organ music started up. Who would have thought a tiny chapel like this would have such a lovely instrument?

David squeezed her knee. "I think that's my cue. You're okay here?"

She nodded. "I'm fine. Go be a groomsman. Or *the* groomsman."

He laughed and kissed her cheek.

It took everything she had not to put her hand over the spot he'd kissed. A shiver worked through her. Did he even realize what he'd done? It had seemed like such a natural response. He took something from Colin as they positioned themselves at the altar, then turned and winked at her. An older woman came down the aisle dressed in a powder blue suit, complete with pill-box hat. The music changed and Jen stood, turning to look.

The bride was resplendent in an ankle-length dress of eyelet lace. The lines were something out of the forties or fifties—very flattering. Though Jen doubted a paper sack would look bad on this woman. She made quick work of the aisle, the older man escorting her was chuckling quietly as he put her hand in Colin's, then stepped to the side and took the hand of the bridesmaid—matron? Did you call them a bridesmatron? Or was every married woman in a wedding party the matron of honor? Why was she even thinking about it? It didn't matter.

Jen sat back down and watched David as the minister began the ceremony. He must have felt her eyes on him. He turned and smiled in her direction. Before long, Rachel and Colin had said their vows and the minister was pronouncing them husband and wife. She clapped as they kissed, her gaze darting to David.

The bridesmaid grabbed Rachel in a tight hug. The man followed suit. Rachel laughed, one hand holding tight to Colin's. Jen stood and crossed her arms. Why was she here? This was a time for family and good friends.

Rachel broke away from the older couple and crossed to Jen. "Hi, I'm Rachel. David said he was bringing someone, so, being full of good deductive reasoning, I'm assuming you're Jen?"

"Yes. Hi. Congratulations." Jen extended her hand. "It was a lovely service."

"Thanks. I'm so glad you could come. We thought for a while that some of Colin's friends from his software days would be able to make it, and then we hoped a few of my old friends might come, but that all fell through so we decided we'd just get married now and have a party another time when people could make the trip. This was the best weekend for my aunt and uncle to come in from Ireland. It's a slow time for Aunt Siobhan's B&B, and mine, for that matter. And I'm babbling. Sorry." She glanced up at her new husband and beamed.

"I'm pretty sure you're allowed to babble on your wedding day. Congratulations again. And thanks for letting me come." Jen reached for David's hand and swallowed a contented sigh when he wrapped his fingers around hers.

"Can we take you two to dinner? Did you have something planned? You were a little skimpy on details." David looked between Colin and Rachel, an eyebrow raised in query.

"We weren't sure if you'd have time, with tomorrow being a workday. I know it's a bit of a drive back to Tyson's Corner." Colin moistened his lips and glanced over his shoulder at Rachel's aunt and uncle. "But I'm game for dinner if you all are. The pub's closed on Sundays or I'd suggest we could go there."

"Ha. I wouldn't agree to that anyway. We're in Annapolis, let's go hunt up seafood." David winked at Jen. "But not shellfish."

Jen chuckled. The rest of the heaviness dissipating, at least for now. "I do make exceptions for a real Maryland crabcake."

"Noted. You two know the town better than me at this point—where should we go?"

"You're quiet. You okay?" David glanced over then returned his eyes to the road. It was dark, but at least the traffic on the Beltway wasn't horrible. Yet.

"Yeah, I'm just tired. Friday night and then today was a lot of people interaction for me. Which sounds dumb."

"No, I get it. I need that recoup time too. Sure that's all?"

Was it? The conversation with Sarah on Friday still bothered her. And today had been another couple choosing a small wedding rather than some extravagant dream. Was one better than the other? "Just thinking about weddings, I guess."

"With so many friends getting married this year, that's not hugely surprising. Anything in particular?"

How much to tell. Was it betraying a confidence to mention the conversation with Amy and the rest of the girls? "On Friday, we talked about weddings some. Amy's trying to get started with her planning 'cause she wants this big, elegant affair. Maybe I'm weird, but I never really had the million-dollar fantasy, you know? I want more than just some random date of my groomsman, mind you, but...it feels like the older I get, the less I worry about the wedding. Are those huge events we see on TV just for young people?"

"I don't know about that. Maybe they're more for people who have a different view of marriage."

"What do you mean?"

David flicked on the turn signal and changed lanes. "As our culture puts more and more emphasis on the party and then ends up with relationships that are over before the bills are paid, I think some Christians are starting to realize we need to get back to focusing on the covenant of marriage. And that doesn't need a party—in fact, sometimes the party detracts from it."

"So you think big weddings are bad?"

"No. Not at all. Not if you can have one in a sane way—not going into huge debt for it, for example. If you can afford it and it's what you want, and you can stay true to God's other commandments for as long as it takes to pull one off, then hey, go nuts. But if any of those things aren't true? Why not have a small wedding and put the focus on the vows you're making? You can always have a big party down the road."

Jen smiled. "That's what I said to Amy. I, uh, guess she and Zach are having some temptation issues."

David nodded. "He mentioned that. Make sense. It's a tough situation to be in."

That was the truth. What must it be like? Would it be similar, down the road, for her and David? They worked in the same building and already she got chills whenever he was near. When he'd kissed her cheek...well, what would a real kiss be like? It had always been relatively simple when she was in college. Somehow, being young and committed to purity was easier then. Now almost everyone she knew believed like Sara, that staying pure was an old fashioned and unrealistic idea. Maybe her other Christian acquaintances weren't as straightforward about it as Sara had been but, if you paid attention, you could tell from the comments they made.

Sometimes she was convinced her mother even thought she was taking it too far.

"Here we are." David turned the car into a space near her apartment door and shifted into park. "Thanks again for coming with me. I had a really good time."

"Me too." Jen reached for the door.

David switched off the engine and touched her arm. "Hang on, I'll walk you to the door."

She smiled and waited as he hopped out and rounded the car to open her door. "Thanks."

He took her hand in his and squeezed.

Jen dug out her keys and stood in front of her apartment. "I guess I'll see you tomorrow?"

"I hope so. Though I'm going to have meetings most of the day. Text me when you're heading to lunch, I'll see if I can break free."

Her heart sank. It was silly. She'd spent time with him today. But she looked forward to their lunches and just seeing him. It was the bright spot to her day. "Okay."

David reached up and brushed a tendril of hair away from her face, tucking it behind her ear. He left his hand curved under her jaw as he slowly leaned forward. His lips were just the whisper of a touch on hers. She shivered and gripped his waist, returning the kiss and pulling him closer. Every contact point was aflame. The world seemed to spin.

David eased back.

Jen pressed her lips together, savoring the tingling.

"I should go." David kissed her forehead.

Jen nodded, not trusting her voice. She unlocked her door and pushed it open. "Tomorrow?"

"Yeah." His voice was husky. "'Night, Jen. Sweet dreams."

That wasn't likely to be a problem.

18

David hunched his shoulders under his mother's gaze.

"You need to bring her to dinner. It's time. From what Ji's said, it's maybe past time."

He frowned. "What do you mean? We've been out a few times with friends, but only on two real dates. And one was a disaster."

"Doesn't matter. You're half in-love with her. I can see it."

Heat crawled up the back of his neck as a denial formed on his lips. Except...was he? "I don't think—"

"Of course not. You haven't realized it. Take it from your mother, though, you are. And so, I want to meet her." His mom smiled and patted his hand. "Bring her on Saturday. We'll have Ji and Min over and no one else. That way it won't be as intimidating."

David scoffed. Limiting it to his parents and older sister wasn't exactly keeping it laid back. His other siblings—combined— would put Jen through less of a gauntlet. Though maybe, having already had lunch with Ji, it wouldn't be quite so bad. It wasn't like he had a choice. Mom was clearly intent on getting her way. "I'll ask if she's free."

"She will be. If she doesn't see what she has in you, then she's not good enough."

"Mom."

"What? It's true. You're a good son, a good man. You deserve someone who recognizes that."

Unlike Soo. That was the unspoken finish to the sentence. His parents had been more upset than him when they broke up, but once they realized he wasn't nearly as hurt as they'd imagined, they acted as if they'd never been in favor of the match. It would be funny if it hadn't made things awkward at church for at least six months. Which was a moot point now. Especially seeing as he was happy at his new church. Having a group of friends there already didn't hurt, but it wouldn't have been enough to keep him if the preaching wasn't solid.

"Tell me about the church you've been attending." His mother settled onto a stool at the kitchen island and patted the spot next to her. "Since you don't come for lunch and I have to bribe you to come over on a Wednesday night, you must be enjoying it."

David chuckled and sat. "Sorry. I keep thinking I'll come to lunch, but there's a group of people I know who go there and they keep inviting me along."

"And Jen is one of them?"

He nodded.

"This is good. You like it, then?"

"I really do. The preaching is so thought-provoking. I find myself thinking about it from one week to the next. The Pastor is focused on what it means to live for Jesus in today's world and having a consistent, visible faith. Even when it's hard, and not what the culture would say is reasonable."

She smiled. "I've heard that. It's nice to have it confirmed. I miss seeing your face, but I think where you are is better for you in the long run. You were never really challenged at our church, were you?"

He shook his head. He hadn't realized that was the case until he tried somewhere else though. How many people stayed where they were comfortable and missed out on the chance to grow?

"Bring this young woman of yours to dinner. Will she eat Korean food?"

"I took her for chicken one lunch. She liked that. She seems pretty adventurous."

"That will make your father happy, though that man loves a hamburger as much as anyone else. Now, tell me about the wedding. Did you take any pictures?"

David dug his phone out of his pocket and opened the photo gallery, offering it to his mother as he started to describe the event.

Back at home, David stretched out on his couch and flipped on the TV. It wasn't too late—not quite nine o'clock. He poked the speed dial he'd set up for Jen and hit mute on the TV remote, letting the police slash forensics team show keep playing in the background with no sound.

"Hi there. I was just thinking about you."

David grinned. "That's nice to hear. Anything specific?"

Jen laughed. "Not really. Just wondering what you were up to. There was a new episode of my favorite cop show on tonight. You mentioned you watch it."

"Yep. It's on right now. I had the DVR start recording, thankfully, since I ended up going to my parents' for dinner and basically just got home."

"Ah. Well, I won't spoil it for you, then, but it's a great episode." She paused and cleared her throat. "How are your parents?"

She sounded nervous. Why? "They're doing well. They are actually hoping we could come for dinner on Saturday."

"Oh. Um. Okay?"

"Great. That's great. I promise it won't be too bad. My sister Ji, you remember her, right?"

"Sure. She had lunch with us. I've been meaning to ask you, was that set up? Or was it really an accident?"

David winced. He'd told Ji that Jen hadn't bought the random bumping into story. "It was arranged. It was that, or this dinner with my parents would've been much sooner.

They're...involved. That's really the best word I can come up with. They're not overbearing or anything, but they like to know what's going on and offer opinions on things. But I promise, they don't care if you don't do what they recommend. They're very firm about their children living their own lives."

"Okay. That actually makes me feel a little better. The questions she asked were...strange for someone who just happened to bump into us."

"I tried to tell her that. She insisted she'd pulled it off. You're not upset?"

"Nah. My parents want to meet you, too."

They did? His stomach jittered. Would they be able to see how he felt as easily as his own parents could? No, of course they wouldn't. It wasn't like he wore his heart on his sleeve. "We can do that, if you want?"

"I'll talk to them and set something up. Probably not for this weekend."

He chuckled, the tension in his shoulders easing. "That's a good idea. So. Saturday. Ji and her husband Min will be there. That's what I'd started to say. And probably her two kids, unless she gets a sitter. I guess I could've asked about that."

"It doesn't matter. I like kids. And who knows, they might make it less awkward."

David pursed his lips. That was possible. His niece and nephew weren't known for keeping things to themselves. But their naked honesty came across as cute and endearing rather than overly forward. Then again. "That's...debatable. But thank you for being okay with whatever. I'll pick you up at five?"

"Sounds good. I'm already pretty sure I can't do lunch tomorrow. We need to have a brainstorming session—we hit something in the next phase of the deliverable that the guys are struggling to design. I have some ideas, but I need to get them on board."

David rubbed the back of his neck. He hated team meetings like that. "Ugh. I'll be praying for you. Those can be rough. Text me when it's over and let me know how it went?"

"Sure. Now, you should go watch that episode so I can talk to you about it. I'm going to read for a little before calling it a night."

He smiled. Her voice had grown soft, warmer somehow. "Okay. 'Night."

Half in love with her. Was his mother right? That seemed...fast. And yet, at the same time, right. They weren't kids, fresh out of college—heck, even in college. He was pushing thirty, she was only what, two years behind him? At some point, did you just realize things were right without all the mucking around?

Lord, would you let me know—clearly—if this is the way you want things to be progressing? Give me the patience and compassion to weather her depression, and to help her when it hits. Help me to have the right words—or the ability to stay silent, whatever she needs. And help her team to see and accept her ideas tomorrow. Amen.

David swallowed, but it did nothing to ease the desert in his mouth. "You look amazing. You didn't have to dress up for this."

Jen smoothed a hand down the knee-length black skirt she wore. "Is it too much? I could go put on slacks. Or jeans. You're wearing khakis."

He was. He'd dressed up a little, though khakis and a sweater was still casual. Of course, he'd dressed up for her, not his parents. He suspected the opposite was true of Jen. "Like I said, amazing. Ready?"

She smiled, her cheeks pinking prettily. "I guess."

"You don't need to be nervous." He had that covered for both of them.

"I'll remind you of that when it's your turn. Speaking of which, what does next weekend look like for you?"

David fought a wince. It was only fair. But still. "I can make that work. Just tell me when."

"All right. I think my folks will want to go out. Mom isn't the best cook. She can handle simple things, but I don't think she'd be confident enough for meeting you the first time." Her hand flew to her mouth. "But don't tell her I said that."

"Your secret's safe with me." He backed out of the parking space, shifted into drive, and reached over to take her hand. "I'm sorry the week got so busy. I hoped we'd be able to have lunch yesterday. Did you have a good time last night with Amy and Sara?"

She shrugged. "I guess. I'm not sure Amy's going to want to hang out with us again. Especially if Paige and Rebecca aren't there. Sara...needs prayer. That's all I can think to say."

"What's going on?" David glanced over before changing lanes.

"She's never made a big secret out of the fact that she isn't as committed to abstinence as I am." A blush stole over her cheeks and she cleared her throat. "But I never expected her to really follow through on it. And she acts like it's no big deal. So she's giving Amy a hard time."

David frowned. "That's rough. What's her reasoning?"

"It's not realistic in today's culture." Jen shook her head. "So I asked her if I could start stealing. After all, people back in Biblical times didn't have as much as we do, so it made sense that we shouldn't steal. But now...it's less realistic. Right?"

David snickered. "How'd that go over?"

"About as well as you think. I got the annoyed, 'It's not the same thing and you know it' defense. And okay, it isn't, but it's close enough. You can't cherry pick what you believe in the Bible. You either take it all or you don't." Jen's hands, which had been gesturing wildly, flopped into her lap. "It's so frustrating."

"You're right. She needs prayer. I'm not sure there's much else you can do if she's not willing to listen to rational thought."

David turned into his parent's driveway and turned off the car. "Here we are. Ready?"

Jen took a deep breath. "Ready as I'm going to be, I think."

19

"That was delicious, Mrs. Pak. Thank you." Jen folded her napkin and set it on her empty plate. In addition to the food being good, the conversation had been pleasant. Less awkward, in fact, than her lunch with David and Ji had been. It was clear Mrs. Pak loved her son. And that David was a little bit of a mama's boy. Since it didn't appear to be extreme, it was kind of cute. "Can I help with the dishes?"

Mrs. Pak grinned but shook her head. "No. I have it. Why don't you and David go sit on the deck. There are enough hints of spring in the air that it should be pleasant. I'll bring out some coffee. You drink coffee?"

Jen nodded.

Mrs. Pak made a shooing motion. "Then go, sit."

"Dinner was good, Mom. Thanks." David shook his head and pushed away from the table, extending his hand to Jen.

Ji looked at her husband. "Feel like some air?"

"Oh. I could use a hand in the kitchen, Ji. Min, you too." Mrs. Pak jerked her head toward the doorway.

Ji snickered as she stood and began collecting plates from the table.

Jen took David's hand and followed him through the living room and out the sliding door onto the deck.

"So?" David settled on the gliding rocker and tugged her hand so she sat beside him.

"They're nice. And dinner really was amazing. You eat like that all the time when you come over?"

He chuckled. "The menu varies. My dad loves to grill, so when the weather's nice, he'll do ribs and burgers."

"Ribs and burgers? Really?"

David nodded. "It's not always Korean barbecue. Though that happens, too. We like all kinds of food around here."

Grasshoppers jumped in her belly. "Did I do okay?"

He squeezed her hand. "You did great. You were you, which is all you needed to be."

She fought the denial that tried to push its way out of her mouth. What did he see in her? She didn't mind—in fact, it left her warm. Could she believe it? Trust him?

"Coffee." Mrs. Pak came out with a tray holding two steaming mugs, a sugar bowl and a pitcher of cream. She set it on the table near the glider and rested a hand on Jen's shoulder. "Thank you for coming. I enjoyed meeting you. I hope it won't be the last time you're here."

"Thank you. I feel the same." Jen smiled.

Approval shone in the older woman's eyes. "I'll leave you to your coffee."

She disappeared back inside and David chuckled and slid his arm around her shoulders. "That's the seal of approval right there. She wouldn't leave us alone if she didn't like you. Or she'd send Dad out here to casually check on us."

She'd passed. Apparently, with flying colors. When was the last time she'd done that? Jen leaned over and pressed a kiss to his cheek.

David turned, his lips meeting hers. Fireworks exploded behind her eyes and her hand moved to his cheek, the tiniest bit of stubble rubbing against her palm. The rest of the world faded from her awareness, leaving just the two of them and their kiss.

Jen's mom opened the door. Her eyes widened and a smile worked its way across her lips. "Baby. It's so good to see you. What brings you by? Come in."

Jen stepped into the house and let Tribble down. The dog yipped and tore off. Her father's laugh echoed out from the den. "Well, dad's happy now. I hadn't seen you in a while. And—even though we've still been talking on the phone, I wanted to apologize for the last time you came over. I handled it badly."

"Oh, baby." Her mom pulled Jen into her arms. "I owe you an apology, too. I know better than to try and throw your depression in your face. But it makes me so mad. Not that you're depressed—that's not your fault—but I don't like to see you hurting, struggling, and I'm helpless to do anything about it. If I could fix it for you, I would. You know that, don't you?"

"I do." Jen eased out of her mom's hug. Honestly, the fact that her mother would fix it was part of the problem. Sometimes she needed that space to try and fix it herself. On the flip side, she could be better about asking for help when she needed it. She didn't have to try and do it all on her own. "Let's go see how many treats dad's given Tribble."

With a laugh, Jen's mom headed toward the den. "You didn't feed her, did you?"

"I gave her breakfast, but maybe she'll skip dinner."

"Skip dinner?" Jen's dad frowned and rubbed Tribble's head. "Such a mean mommy you have, threatening to starve you to death."

Jen chuckled. "Missing one meal, especially after all the treats I know you're going to give her, will not have her wasting away. The vet said she needs to lose three pounds anyway. She's getting chubby."

"She's not. She's perfect. Aren't you?" Dad hugged the dog to his chest, eliciting a yip and frantic face licking. "It's nice to see you, too, though. What brings you by?"

"Can't I just drop by?" Jen settled onto the couch.

"Sure, you can. But you usually don't. Isn't Sunday lunch with friends?" Her dad let go of Tribble and the dog moved to his lap, turning a circle before settling in.

"Yeah. And we had a quick lunch, but everyone was headed in different directions after, so I swung by for Trib and came here. I didn't want to spend the afternoon at home by myself." She'd thought about it, but the walls had started closing in almost immediately. Before the familiar heaviness could settle over her and the tapes of all the things that were wrong with her could start replaying in her mind, she'd grabbed the dog and run for her car. At the time, she hadn't had a destination, but before long, her parent's house had been the obvious choice. The new dose of her medication helped—a lot—but maybe there was no perfect dose that would get her to a place where she was like everyone else.

"Well. I can turn this off and we can play a game, if you want?"

"You don't have to do that, Dad, unless you want to." Jen leaned back. The basketball game didn't hold a lot of interest, but her dad enjoyed it.

"How's your puzzle coming along?" Her mother perched on the edge of her dad's recliner and began petting Tribble.

Jen smiled. She and David had made some progress together. But it still was likely to take her the best part of the year. "It's going. The edges are done, and I'm starting to see some of the picture take shape. It's just good that I don't have a burning desire to host a dinner party anytime soon."

Her mother laughed. "The day you hold a dinner party, I'll...I don't know what I'll do, but it'll be spectacular."

"It could happen." Maybe. Okay, probably not. Jen cleared her throat. "Anyway, you'd mentioned wanting to meet David. Did you still want to do that?"

Her parents stilled and exchanged a look. Her mother spoke first. "You're still seeing him?"

Jen nodded.

"And?"

Jen hunched her shoulders at her father's question. "And what?"

He angled his head to the side. "It's serious?"

"Getting there. I like him a lot. And he...he likes me. He understands the depression."

"He has it too?" Her mother frowned.

"No. His sister has struggled with it though. Most of her life. So he's...amazing."

Dad nodded. "Then I'd like to meet him, yes."

"Me, too. Do you want to bring him over for dinner? Or we could go out? Probably better to go out. I'm not going to win any cooking awards. We all know that." Her mother laughed.

"You're a good cook, Mom. I'm fine with whatever."

"Let's go out. That way your mother doesn't have to get all worked up about what to make and all that."

Her mother grinned. "You know me too well. Choose a place and let us know when to meet you. We'll be there."

"Okay. You're gonna like him." They had to. He was too important for them not to.

"I already do, baby." Her mother reached over and patted her leg. "Now. Basketball or board game?"

"Hey—have a couple of minutes?" David poked his head in Jen's office then frowned and stepped into the room, closing the door behind him. "What's wrong?"

Jen rubbed her eyes and pushed away from her monitor. How did he see her so clearly when no one else noticed a thing? She shrugged. "I don't know. It's just one of those days."

He scooted around her desk and perched on its edge, taking her face in his hands. "I'm sorry. Can I...can I pray for you?"

She blinked. Her chest tightened and hot tears formed behind her eyes. "You'd do that?"

"I already do. Just this time would be in person." He leaned forward and brushed his lips over hers before bowing his head. "Heavenly Father, Jen is one of Your precious daughters and I ask that You would fill her with the tangible knowledge of Your love. Give her peace and comfort and the strength to get through today. Jesus, we ask that You would take her depression from her, but if that's not Your will, we ask that You would surround her with people who understand and will walk alongside her through this trial. In Your name we pray, amen."

"Amen." Jen sniffled as a tear wormed its way down her cheek. "Thank you."

"Any idea why today's so hard?"

She shook her head. If she knew, she'd do something about it. But the wall descended whenever it wanted to. Or so it seemed. Things had been a little better as her new dose built up. And then today—wham—it was back. The heaviness that covered her entire body, the chanting litany of reasons why she'd never be enough, the desperate urge to crawl into bed, pull a pillow over her head, and never resurface. But she'd made herself get up and she'd made it to work. Maybe she wasn't as productive as a normal day, but she could fake it with the best of them. She forced a smile. "Did you have a reason you stopped by?"

He blinked. "Mostly I wanted to say hello. It's been busy again this week and I missed you."

Jen stared at her hands. She's missed him, too, but had convinced herself—or nearly had, at least—that she'd been imagining his feelings for her.

He tipped her chin up and held her gaze. A smile played at the corners of his mouth. "Are you going to make me beg?"

"Beg? For what?"

He shook his head. "You didn't miss me?"

She grinned. "I did. I...it's not silly?"

David shrugged. "I'm not the best person to ask, seeing as how I have a vested interest in your answer, but I'm going to go with no. It's not silly."

Jen hunched her shoulders. Had she ever missed someone when she knew she'd see them on the weekend? None of her previous boyfriends came to mind. Was this...could she be in love with him? It was too soon. Even if it wasn't, she'd keep it to herself. "Okay."

"Even if it is? We can be silly together." David winked and leaned forward to press a brief kiss to her lips, following with another on the tip of her nose. "I should get back upstairs. There's a meeting in..." he glanced at his watch and groaned "six minutes. Call you tonight?"

She nodded. "I'd like that. Thanks. For coming down. For praying. For all of it."

"My pleasure."

20

David skimmed through the email in his personal account. He rarely checked it. His friends and family knew to send something to his work email if they needed him to see it. Or they texted him. That was always better. Most of the email was spam or suggestions of women who might be a good match from the online dating site he'd signed up with. He really should go in and delete that account. What had possessed him to do it in the first place? Desperation. Coupled with a terrible first date. But they were past that now and almost to the place where they could laugh about it.

But he wasn't taking Jen to Shirlington again anytime soon. Just in case.

Could he log in on his phone and just take care of it? He opened the web browser and entered the URL. Download their app? No, thank you. He didn't need to download an app just to delete an account and then have to delete the app. He'd take care of it when he had a minute with his laptop. As it was—his gaze flicked to the clock—he needed to jump in the car and start heading to Jen's. Showing up late to the restaurant where they were meeting her parents was not the impression he wanted to make.

Traffic was about what he expected on a Saturday evening. Not light, but not terrible. He found a parking spot near Jen's apartment and was shifting into park when she stepped out and pulled the door closed behind her. She hurried to his car and wrenched open the passenger side.

"Hi. I'm nervous. I was pacing and driving Tribble up a wall, so when I saw you pull in, I figured I'd let her off the hook and just come out. That's okay, right?"

He reached over and squeezed her hand. "It's fine. This isn't a big deal. It's dinner. Unless you know of some reason why your parents wouldn't like me?"

Jen's laugh bordered on shrill. "No. Of course not. You're amazing. I'm sure they'll love you. It's just that I haven't really brought many guys to meet them. Not guys that matter. They've met guys I know, obviously. When I was in high school, I had friends over all the time. But this is different."

He smiled and kissed her knuckles as warmth spread through him. He was amazing and mattered to her. Even knowing it was early to be trotting out the "L" word didn't stop him from hungering to hear it. And say it. Of course, it wasn't as if there was a schedule somewhere he could print out that told him how long to wait. They'd been seeing each other almost daily since the beginning of the year. It was nearly March. Did the fact that they worked together—and therefore could have lunch together frequently—change anything? He bit back a sigh. Now wasn't the time to be worrying about this. "Where are we meeting again?"

"That went well, I think." David ran his knuckles lightly down Jen's cheek as they stood by her apartment door. "Is your dad always so funny, or was he trying to ease tension?"

Jen fumbled her keys. "A little of both, I think. Do you want to come in? I could make some tea? I don't have decaf or I'd offer coffee."

"Okay." He didn't want tea. But he also wasn't ready to put an end to their evening. They'd had dinner and dessert in record time for a Saturday night. And their server had clearly been in a hurry to turn the table, so they hadn't lingered. Which had them back at Jen's before seven-thirty. He followed her in and pushed the door closed before tucking his hands into his pockets. It was that or reach for her and kiss her like he'd been imagining all evening. And that wasn't a particularly productive train of thought to encourage.

Tribble bounded from the kitchen and stood, quivering, at the sliding glass door. Jen followed on her heels. "I need to let her out for a minute. Wanna come? Or you can wait here. We won't be long."

David reached out and took her hand. "I'll come. It's a nice night."

They stood on the patio while Tribble frolicked in the grass and did her business. It wasn't cold, but February wasn't leaving without one last little bite of winter in the air.

Jen leaned against him. "It's getting cold. Hurry, Trib."

He slipped his arm around her and tugged her closer. "But the moon is amazing. Look at it."

She lifted her face to the sky where the nearly-full orb glowed silver. "Oh, it's lovely."

"You're lovely."

Pink spilled across her cheeks. "I don't know what to say when you say that."

He leaned in and brushed a kiss over her lips. "That's okay."

Tribble dashed over and began yipping while running circles around their ankles. Jen laughed. "I think she's ready to go in."

David chuckled. "Looks like it."

Back in Jen's living room, David sat while Jen took Tribble into the kitchen for a treat and to get the tea. When she came back, she set two steaming mugs on the coffee table and settled next to him. "What now? Want to see if there's a movie on?"

A movie was a good idea. Wasn't it? He'd have to keep in mind that they were both headed to church in the morning. And they needed to be able to go with a clean conscience. He could do that. "Sure. But before we do that, can I ask you something?"

She turned, her eyebrows lifting. "Of course."

"You're not in Paige and Jackson's wedding, right?"

"I'm manning the guest book."

"Not a bridesmaid?"

Jen shook her head. "Thankfully, no. That whole three times a bridesmaid thing has long since passed me by, but I try not to add on too many extra numbers if I can avoid it. They're just having Ben and Zach and Amy and Rebecca. Why?"

"I was hoping you'd go with me?"

She grinned. "Absolutely."

He let out a breath. "Great. So, what kind of movie are we talking about?"

21

The pounding on the door set Tribble barking. She raced to the door, abandoning her half-full bowl of kibble. Jen sighed and put her bowl of soup on top of the magazine she was reading. Why didn't people call before coming over in the middle of the week? It wouldn't be David. He was on another proposal team and would be working crazy nights all week. Mom usually called first. Which left who? She shuffled to the door and peeked out. Sara.

"Hey. What's wrong?" Jen pushed the door wider to let a sobbing mess of running eyeliner masquerading as her friend come in.

Sara made a bee-line for the couch and collapsed on to it, her chest heaving.

Jen sat next to her and rubbed her arm. "Hey. Hey. What happened? You have to calm down and tell me what's going on."

"He got married." Sara took a shuddering breath that ended in a sob.

What? "Who? You're not making any sense."

"Luc. He got married. Here." Sara dragged her arm across her nose, smearing snot and mascara on her sleeve and cheek before digging her phone out of her pocket. She tapped the screen and offered the phone to Jen.

Jen looked at the text message, complete with a photo of Luc and a smiling woman who was nearly his height standing on the beach in formal attire. "Oh, sweetie. I'm sorry. He didn't say anything?"

Sara shook her head and put her phone back in her pocket. "Now what do I do?"

That was a question Jen wasn't going to be able to answer. So many different options presented themselves. But now probably wasn't the time for a lecture on why not having slept with him would've made this easier. "Maybe you should take some time to get over him before doing anything?"

"I guess. But I don't want to go to the wedding alone. You want to come with me? Just go together, no dates?"

Jen winced. She didn't want to extinguish the tiny glint of hope in her friend's eyes, but...she cleared her throat. "I'm going with David. He already asked. I'm sorry. You can hang with us though."

"Oh, sure. I can be a third wheel. I could do that with Rebecca and Ben." A hint of a whine entered her friend's voice. "Can't you tell him something came up?"

"No. But we'll figure something out. You want to hang here tonight? I can make up the couch and we can stay up and watch a movie. I think I even have ice cream."

Sara blinked. "Really?"

"Absolutely. Come on, I'll find you some pajamas."

Jen scooted to the middle of the pew where the gang usually sat. How she'd managed to be the first person there was anyone's guess, but she'd take it. She set her purse on the floor and turned sideways in the seat to watch the door. She and David had gone to dinner on Friday night in Occoquan, a little historic town south on I-95, though still well within the general suburban sprawl of Northern Virginia. But Occoquan itself was a tiny oasis in the midst of that. And the French restaurant tucked behind trees and other houses-turned-shops was an amazing eating experience. The walk along the quaint main street, that was bordered on one side by the river, had been a perfect ending to the evening. They'd gotten together with

Jackson, Ben, and Rebecca last night and played a board game at the restaurant while Paige dropped by periodically with food. In all, an amazing weekend. Topping it off with worship was...perfect.

"How'd you get here so early?"

Jen started and turned, laughing, to see David. "You snuck up on me? You never use a different door."

He grinned and pressed a quick kiss to her cheek. "Gotta keep you on your toes. Question stands. I thought I was an early riser."

"Believe me, this is unusual. Tribble had an upset stomach. She was pacing and moaning most of the night, so when the clock finally hit six-thirty, I called it a night and got up."

David frowned. "Is she okay?"

Sweet man. Jen shrugged. "She ate her breakfast and her morning business seemed normal. So I think so. She probably ate something. I don't always catch her before she gets to something when she's out on the grass. If she's at it again this afternoon though, I'll call the vet tomorrow."

The rest of the crew—with the notable exception of Sara—filed in.

Rebecca leaned forward and met Jen's gaze. "Where's Sara? She wasn't there last night, and not here today?"

Jen frowned. She wasn't here *yet*. But maybe she'd still make it? "Have you heard from her this week at all?"

Rebecca shook her head.

"If she doesn't show, I'll talk to you after the service." Jen leaned back as the praise band started the first song. Should she mention Sara's breakup to everyone or wait and let Sara do it? Maybe just tell Rebecca privately? She clenched her hands into fists.

David reached over and took her hand in his. Jen forced her fingers to relax and focused on the music, sending up a prayer for guidance. If Sara was drifting into depression from Luc's actions—and why wouldn't she be?—Didn't Jen owe it to her to do what she could to try and help? She knew depression too well to let someone she loved suffer without trying.

Jen almost laughed when Pastor Brown asked people to turn to Romans twelve, and focus on verses nine through twenty-one. Her eyes filled with tears as he came to the portion about weeping with those who weep. She squeezed David's hand. He was the first person who'd been willing to do that with her. And while, sure, maybe Paul was talking about people weeping because of actual hardship or grief, clinical depression wasn't a picnic. Having someone willing to walk alongside her, to hold her hand and not tell her to just buck up and smile, but to simply sit with her? There simply weren't words for how much that helped.

As the end-of-service music started, she turned to David. "Thank you."

One corner of his mouth quirked up, a question in his eyes. "For what?"

"Just being you."

The smile spread into a grin. "That's easy. But you're welcome. Have time for lunch?"

She pulled her lower lip between her teeth. "I want to say yes, but I'm worried about Sara. I was sure she'd get here—but since she didn't come out last night and isn't here now, I think maybe I should go check on her."

"What's going on?" Rebecca leaned around David, her expression worried.

Jen sighed. "Apparently Luc got married and texted her his wedding photo. Then, not much after that, he was texting to let her know when he'd be in town again and asking if their plans were still on."

"He didn't." Fury flared in Ben's eyes and he growled. "If he hadn't already been fired, I'd go make sure it happened."

"He got fired? When was that?" Sara hadn't said anything about that on Tuesday night when she was over. Surely she would have if she'd known.

"Friday. I'm not one hundred percent on the details, but my understanding is that he's been on probation for a while now for hooking up with women at the various job sites he goes to." Ben winced. "I think I might have mentioned the thing with Sara where it was overheard and that pushed it over the edge. At this point, I just feel bad that I didn't know and had him at the wedding. I thought he was just a co-worker who ended up with the bad luck to be away from home over Christmas."

"You were trying to do a nice thing, honey, it's okay." Rebecca patted Ben's knee. "I wonder if Sara knows the last part?"

Jen shrugged. "Want to come with me and check on her?"

Holding two takeout bags in one hand, the giant sodas wedged in the crook of her arm, Jen banged on Sara's apartment door, counted to twenty, then banged again. The sound of the TV inside lessened and, just as she was getting ready to pound on the door a third time, the door opened a tiny crack.

"What?" Only half of Sara's face was visible through the tiny space, but her eyes were red and swollen and her cheek was blotchy.

"Oh, sweetie. He's not worth this. Let me in. I brought your favorite." Jen nodded to the bags of greasy pseudo-Mexican food.

With a sigh, Sara opened the door wider. "Did you get the thing where they glue the two tacos together with nacho cheese?"

Jen pretended to gag as she nodded. "Only because I love you. If they contaminate my normal taco, I'm going to be annoyed."

A ghost of a smile hovered around Sara's lips. "Come on. We can eat in the kitchen. I should probably spend a few minutes in an upright position today."

Jen carried the takeout to the kitchen and set it down on the island before hopping on to one of Sara's stools.

"Did you know they fired him?" Sara dug through the bags, pulling out the combined tacos, sauce packets, and a bag of fried dough. "That's my fault, apparently."

"Says who?"

Sara nodded to her phone, which sat on the charging station at the end of the island. Jen unplugged it and handed it to her friend. Sara poked the surface a few times before sliding it back to Jen.

Jen scanned the texts, each one increasingly angry and foul. The last one made her cringe. She hit the power button to turn off the screen. "You blocked him, right?"

"Yeah, for all the good it does. He stopped texting and started calling. I added him to the auto reject list, but it still wore my battery down. And I don't know how to delete voicemail without listening to at least a little of it."

Jen reached into the bag and took out the two plain tacos she'd gotten for herself. "Could you call your provider? Maybe they can wipe it for you?"

"Maybe. I guess I can look into that tomorrow."

"Or, if you want, you can dial in and put in your password and I'll do it. Once the code's in, you can leave the room so you don't accidentally overhear anything."

"You'd do that for me?"

Jen nodded.

"Okay. Later though."

Should she mention that Ben said Luc had been on probation? It might ease the guilt that it was clear Sara was feeling. Even if it was unjustified. On the other hand, that would mean admitting they'd talked about her—it—and, while she hadn't promised she wouldn't, it seemed like something that was better left to Sara to explain. Jen sighed. Why did everything have to be so complicated?

Sara frowned at her. "Spill it."

Jen tried for innocence. "What?"

"Please. You look guilty. What did everyone say?" Sara crunched into her food, nacho cheese oozing out the sides and onto her fingers.

"Ben said that he just found out that Luc had been on probation for a while. So you're absolutely not responsible for him getting fired. That was on its way."

Sara wiped the cheese off her fingers. "Why was he on probation? Luc said they loved him."

"He did good work, maybe. Ben said that was true. But...I guess he was picking up girlfriends at every project. Sometimes more than one."

Sara closed her eyes, her whole body shrinking in on itself. "So I'm just one of many? Not special at all...despite what he said?"

Jen chewed on her lip as she nodded. "Apparently. I'm so sorry."

"Not your fault. Totally all my fault." Sara pushed the taco away and reached for her soda. "You can say it. I deserve to have you say it."

"Say what?"

"I told you so. Aren't you dying to say 'I told you so'?"

Her heart sank. She turned to face Sara. "No. That would imply I'm happy this happened to you. And I'm not. Why would you think I was?"

"Don't you think I deserve it? After all, I chose to sleep with him—not that I was some kind of blushing virgin to start out with. So isn't this God's fit punishment or something?"

Jen took a long drink of soda, her heart breaking for her friend. "I...don't think God works that way. Yes, there are consequences for sin. Any sin, mind you. But I don't think God's up there with a big flyswatter eagerly waiting to whap us when we screw up. If He was, there would be no reason for Him to have sent Jesus. Why would He offer forgiveness and mercy if He enjoyed punishing us?"

Sara looked away. "I keep waiting for Him to give up on me, just like everyone does eventually."

"God never gives up on us, Sara. Even when we think He's gone and we're alone in the dark, He's there. If anything, we don't see Him because we're not bothering to look."

22

"You're here again?" Ji laughed as she opened the door and let David in. "What is it this time?"

David hunched his shoulders and tucked his hands in his pockets. "I can go. Ask Mom, maybe."

"No. I'm giving you a hard time. You know that. Come on in." Ji closed the door and flipped the lock. "Want to sit in the living room?"

David listened. It was quiet. Usually at this time of night, the kids were tearing around the house and Ji and Min were desperately trying to wrangle them into bed. "Where is everyone?"

"There's some production at the kids' school. I had a late meeting, so knew I was going to miss most of it. Min went. He's recording it for me. I got home about ten minutes ago and they should be home in the next half hour. So, enjoy the quiet while you can." Ji collapsed into a chair and propped her feet on the matching ottoman.

David paced across the room and stood in front of the array of photos that adorned the long wall of the room. "When is too soon to tell someone you love them? Or to be in love with them, even? Or think you are?"

"There are a lot of questions in there. Which one are we tackling?"

He turned, frowning. "How do you know you're in love?"

"You were in love with Soo, weren't you? So you know."

He shook his head. He'd said he was in love with her, yes. But actually in love? Compared to how he felt about Jen—how he felt when he was around her, how he missed her when she wasn't there—what he'd felt for Soo was nothing. "I'm not sure I do."

Ji sighed. "Sit down. You're making me nervous."

With a strangled laugh, David sat. "Better?"

"A little. Not really. Relax. I'm going to tell you a secret that I'm only just beginning to understand after being married for a while. Being in love isn't something that happens to you, it's something you choose. I know it's hokey, but if you look at First Corinthians thirteen, you really do see a picture of what day-to-day love is. It's not the electricity at their touch or the ache when they're away, though those are good things. It's whether or not you're willing to choose to be patient, kind, humble, and always seek her best interest over your own. If you're ready to protect, trust, hope, and persevere no matter what in order to have her in your life, then you love her. And there will be days, I promise you, that you're going to have to work extra hard to choose those things. Is she worth the work?"

David closed his eyes. Was Jen worth it? Easy. Yes. Even on her bad days, when you could see her depression closing around her like a fog, he wanted to be there with her—for her. "She is."

Ji smiled. "Congratulations, little brother. You're in love."

He snickered. "So when is it okay to say that?"

"I can't help you with that one. I don't think there's a set schedule. Some people find love quickly. Others take a long time to see it. Or they see it, but avoid it for a while before embracing it. You're old enough to know what you're about, though. Neither of you are teenagers. So, depending on what you think comes after you tell her that, then I'd say go for it."

"What do you mean?"

"Why do you want to say 'I love you'? What's next?"

David squirmed. Wasn't it enough to be in love? At least for a little while? "Marriage, eventually. I hope."

Ji nodded. "Good answer."

"What did you think I was going to say?"

"Exactly what you said. But there are some guys who use I love you as a hammer. I wanted to make sure you hadn't become one of them."

Like he'd tell his sister if he only wanted to say the words to try and talk Jen into bed? And if Ji knew Jen at all, she'd know it wouldn't work anyway. Her clear, strong position on that was something he not only agreed with but admired. "Sadly, I'm still the charming boy next door who many see as too mild to possibly be interesting enough to date."

She laughed. "How many women do you need in your life? You found one who's happy to date you, who you're in love with. Be okay with that."

"I am. Just had to try and get a little sympathy. Never did work on you."

Ji tossed a pillow at him.

David caught it and tucked it behind his back, the tension in his shoulders and neck easing. He was in love with Jen. And it was time she knew.

"You're getting to be a regular around here." Ben flipped his book closed as David plopped down next to him.

"Can't beat the food. Even if you do have to deal with the heat of the kitchen and all the banging. How does Paige stand it?" David looked at Jackson.

"She thrives on it. I don't get it, but it works for her. Really well." Jackson grinned and pushed his own pile of work away. "Zach's on his way out, too. I guess Amy got dragooned into whatever the women are up to tonight."

"Too bad Paige couldn't get the night off." David frowned. Did Paige mind getting left out of these things? They should try and schedule around her nights off, or when the restaurant was closed.

Though from everything he'd observed, Paige lived and breathed Season's Bounty. Maybe she liked having the built-in excuse?

Jackson sighed. "I tried to convince her. But with the wedding next weekend and taking a week off for our honeymoon, she didn't want to. I think she's more comfortable with being away for a week since her dad will be here. When she grabs a random night off, it's just Hector in charge. And as much as she trusts him, she doesn't like leaving her baby."

"Does it bother you?" David rested his elbows on the table. He was used to a pretty standard work week. As was Jen. Though with the proposals that Kurt kept dropping on him, his evenings and weekends were being eaten up more lately than in the past. Jen understood. Was it the same dynamic?

Jackson shook his head. "Nah. She puts up with my weird hours during elections. It's the give and take of a relationship. If she didn't love her job, maybe it would bother me from that standpoint. But as it is? Nope."

"Rebecca and you both have the same hours, basically, don't you?" David shifted so he could see Ben and include in him in the conversation.

"Generally. Sometimes she ends up with a Saturday shift or a slightly later night, but it's not a big deal. When we have a big project or fundraising effort gearing up, she has to deal with fluctuation in my schedule. It's not a big deal. You having trouble with Jen?"

"No. At least, not that I know about." David grinned. "Just been doing a lot of thinking about what makes a relationship work, long term."

"Aha." Jackson and Ben exchanged a look. "Will we be hearing wedding bells for the two of you in the future?"

David hunched his shoulders. "That might be a bit premature."

"What's premature? Not me. I'm late. As usual, since moving to D.C. And that is, hands down, the worst thing about living downtown and having friends in the suburbs." Zach slid into the seat next to Jackson. "Hey, David. You lose all your other friends?"

David snickered as Jackson punched Zach's arm. "Sort of. The more I hang out with you, the more I realize those guys weren't really my scene. There's no room for someone with a serious relationship in that crew. Most of the guys who get married—or even just have a steady girlfriend—drift off. Used to annoy me, but I understand it more now."

Zach grinned. "So, you and Jen are serious?"

David nodded, but was saved from Zach's follow-on question by Paige.

"Here's a handsome group. Gazpacho to start tonight—it's March, it's supposed to be spring, even if the weather hasn't completely gotten the memo. And spring is just a hop, skip, and jump from summer. So, time to try out some cold soup recipes and see what makes the cut. I promise the rest of the food will be warm." She laughed as she set down four bowls, dropped a handful of spoons on the table, and disappeared back into the cooking area.

"How serious?" Zach dipped his spoon into the bowl in front of him and blew across the contents.

David snickered as he pulled a bowl closer. "You realize gazpacho is cold. Right?"

"Whatever, it's soup. The habit is ingrained. And you're avoiding the question."

Jackson nodded. "Zach has a point. That's twice you've dodged the question."

Ben lifted a finger. "I concur. What's the deal?"

"I'm in love with her." David swallowed the lump in his throat. It was the first time he'd said it, that plainly, out loud. He'd danced around it when he talked to his sister, but that wasn't the same as throwing it out there.

"Congrats, man." Zach reached across the table for a fist bump.

David tapped his knuckles to Zach's, then Jackson's and Ben's. But he wasn't sure celebration was the correct response. "Yeah, well, don't break out the wedding favors just yet. I haven't told her. And I don't know if she feels the same way."

"I'm guessing she does."

David turned to look at Ben. "Why?"

"Little things Rebecca has said. Nothing concrete, mind you, but I'd say the chance of her returning your feelings are high."

"Still, at some point you have to go out on a limb and take the first step, right?" Zach smiled before scraping the bottom of his bowl.

David sighed. They were probably right. But wasn't it supposed to be a big occasion when you did that? Shouldn't it be memorable? He'd have to consider the options and put a plan into place.

"Now that we've settled that." Jackson pushed his empty bowl into the center of the table and pinned Zach with his gaze. "What have you decided?"

Zach shook his head. "I don't know. Nothing, I guess. We've been talking to her parents some, they tend to agree with you all that we should get married and plan a party for later. I'm fine with that, but Amy is hesitant. She still has that dream, you know, big white dress, everyone around looking at her. I guess it doesn't count if you're already married when it happens."

David frowned and finished his soup. It just kept getting more and more complicated, didn't it? You managed to find someone, fall in love and realize you wanted to spend the rest of your life with them and then, suddenly, you're faced with a wedding that takes on a life of its own, all because little girls are fed wedding propaganda from the moment they get their first doll.

"Any idea what it'd take to convince her? I mean, Paige and I were dancing around that whole issue until you put everything into perspective for us. Any way for us to return the favor?" Jackson stacked the empty bowls in the middle of the table now that everyone was finished.

Zach shrugged. "Wish I knew. Just pray for us."

"You can always hang out at the house. Jason and Karin aren't going to be back until May, so the place is still ours 'til then. I can leave some of my stuff, so you're not crashing on the floor."

"Thanks, Jackson. I appreciate it. I don't think it'll come to that. At least, I hope not. At this point, the thing I really love about where I live is the commute. And the apartment is fantastic. It's stretching my resolve, though, to be that close to Amy all the time. I never thought I'd even consider the things that I'm thinking these days." Zach ran a hand through his hair.

"I'll keep praying." Jackson reached for his phone as it chimed. He laughed. "Paige says she hasn't forgotten about us, but that it's going to be a few more minutes. So, Ben, what's new with you?"

23

"No. I don't need your pity." Sara sighed and flopped back on Jen's couch. Tribble jumped up and curled into a ball next to her. She smiled and rubbed the dog's head. "I'll find a date. Or go stag. I'm secure enough to do that, right?"

Jen stayed quiet. Did Sara want an honest answer or affirmation? Because secure wasn't a word she'd usually use in conjunction with Sara. Why did Rebecca always manage to leave before conversations like this started? It was like she had a conversational radar that warned her it was time to flee.

"All right, fine. I'm not. But I'm working on it, does that count?"

Jen grinned. "Of course it does. Maybe the wedding is a good opportunity for you to do that."

"Funny. A wedding is not the place to try and work on dateless comfort. Nobody goes to a wedding alone. So it's not like I could meet someone there."

"I'm not sure that's true. You hear all kinds of stories of people who met their spouse at a wedding. Going alone might not be too bad." If you wanted to put a fine point on it, she and David had met at a wedding. But it wasn't probably a good idea to bring that up. It was liable to remind Jen of Luc, and that was the last thing she needed to do.

"You know, I've never done online dating. There are a few places that are geared toward Christians. Maybe I should try that."

Jen winced. The whole idea of online dating left a sour taste in her mouth. She hadn't done it, but it just seemed so...ridiculous.

"Really? You don't know anyone you could ask to go to the wedding? Not even as friends? There's got to be someone at church..."

Sara sighed. "There isn't. That's the problem. I don't have many guy friends—maybe because I end up dating them and then it ends and it's weird. For that matter, you and Rebecca are my main girl friends. And it's not like either of you are going to hook me up with someone. Rebecca's fiancé's roommates are both engaged and David just hangs out with us—does he even have other friends?"

David had a lot of friends. Maybe not best-buddy kinds of friends, but it seemed like everyone at the office knew him in one way or another. And the Korean church he went to before switching wasn't exactly small. Surely there were single people there? She couldn't fathom the idea that he'd been spending nights and weekends at home before they started dating. "He has to have some kind of group. I haven't met them, but that doesn't mean they don't exist."

Sara scoffed. "No. But it means they're either not worth knowing or he's embarrassed to introduce you for some reason."

"Or that they're not the kind of friends who do things with dates. You know as well as I do that there are some groups of women who you just don't bring a guy to the stuff they do."

"True. Though I'm kind of surprised you know that. You've never been one to hang with that kind of group."

Jen smiled. "Just because I don't fit in with them, doesn't mean I don't know about them. I could ask Braedon. He's pretty nice."

"Who's Bradeon?"

"Guy on my team at work. I don't think he's seeing anyone." She didn't know for sure. How awkward was that conversation going to be if she was wrong? Maybe she should've kept her mouth shut.

"What's he look like?"

Ugh. What a horrible question. He looked like Braedon. "I don't know. Kind of average? Brown hair, brown eyes, taller than me."

"Let's hope you're never mugged. The police won't know what to do with you. Got a picture of him on your phone?"

Jen frowned. "Why would I have a picture of a coworker on my phone?"

Sara closed her eyes. "Just...never mind. I'll try the online thing. We'll hold Brandon—"

"Bradeon."

"Brandon, Braedon, whatever. We'll hold him in reserve."

"Free for lunch?" David grinned as he leaned in the doorway to her office.

Jen's heart sank. "Aw, man. I wish I was. I promised Rebecca and Sara I'd drive out. Sara has some huge news that she can only share with us in person. She sounded really upset, but no matter how I tried to pry details out of her, she said it had to be in person. I was just getting ready to leave."

"Bummer. Can I walk down to your car with you?"

"Absolutely." Jen locked her computer and grabbed her purse, her whole body lighter than it had been even five minutes ago. David had that effect on her. It was one of the things she loved about him. She stopped, swallowing, as it hit her. She loved him.

"You okay?" David's face was filled with concern.

She smiled and hoped it didn't look as wobbly as her insides were. "Yeah. Yeah, I am."

He drew his eyebrows together and studied her for a moment before offering his hand. "Ready, then?"

She twined her fingers through his. Love. With a capital L. Butterflies swooped in her stomach. Should she tell him? No. Not at work. Maybe...maybe at the wedding? There wasn't going to be a fancy reception—just cake and light snacks in the fellowship hall after the ceremony—but there'd probably still be a good time, a romantic time, to mention it. And then hope he felt the same way.

"So you don't have any idea if Sara's news is good or bad?"

Jen pulled her thoughts back under control and shook her head. "From the tone of her voice, I'm leaning toward bad. Or bad-ish."

He laughed. "Bad-ish? Where does that fall on the bad scale?"

"I don't know, less than epic disaster, but mostly bad with some element that still has the potential for working out for the best in the long run?"

"You've thought through that bad-ish scale, haven't you?"

Jen chuckled. "Maybe a little. I like to have definitions for things."

David held the elevator door for her then punched the button for the garage. "It's always good to know what things mean. And be able to define them for the rest of us. Lunch tomorrow?"

The elevator dinged as it stopped at the garage level. Jen nodded. "I'd like that."

"Cool." He tucked his hands in his pockets and walked beside her as she wove through the parked cars to hers. When she clicked the unlock button, he pulled open the door and leaned against it as she slid behind the wheel. "Maybe this is weird, but I'll miss you."

Jen grinned. "Call me tonight?"

He leaned in and kissed her. "Absolutely."

"Finally. What took you so long?" Sara jumped up from the table, grabbed Jen by the hand, and dragged her to the table. Rebecca was already picking at the foot-long sandwich in front of her.

"Do I get to buy a sandwich first?" Jen yanked her hand away from Sara. "It can't be so important that I have to starve."

"Fine. Go get food. But hurry." Sara glared at Jen.

What was going on? This wasn't the distraught Sara she'd expected. So...maybe the news wasn't personal? But then, what could it be? It had to be more about Luc. Jen ordered her sandwich, paid, and filled her cup at the soda machine before making her way to the back table. She set her food down and sat. "All right, what's going on?"

Sara tapped her phone and slid it across the table to Jen.

Furrowing her brow, Jen picked up the phone and looked at the photo of David—it was the same one on the company website. "I don't understand. What is this?"

"The Christian dating site I signed up with."

David was on a dating site? Her heart sped up. "Maybe it's from a long time ago?"

Sara shook her head.

Rebecca reached for the phone and pinched the screen to enlarge it, winced, and handed it back. "Not really. Look where it says 'Member since'."

Jen took the phone and stared at it. That was...right after their first date. Her thoughts shattered into a thousand directions, along with pieces of her heart. She pushed away from the table, her chair clattering to the floor. Unable to see through the tears blurring her eyes, she grabbed her purse and turned toward the door. "I have to go."

24

David frowned at his phone and poked redial. Why wasn't she answering? He'd swung by her office on his way home, thinking maybe they could grab some supper, but she was already gone. Or, if he was worried about accuracy, the guys on her team said she'd never come back from lunch. She'd called and said she wasn't feeling well. Did she get food poisoning?

Her phone went to voicemail again and he sighed. "Jen, it's me—David—again. Are you okay? The guys on your team said you never made it back from lunch. I could bring some soup over? Give me a call, please, and let me know you're okay."

He ended the call and dropped his phone on the nightstand. There was no point in texting. He'd tried that already, too. No response. *Dear Jesus, please help her to be okay. And help me not to worry. Please.*

His gut twisted. What was he supposed to do now? If she didn't call back, he couldn't keep bugging her, could he? Should he drive over? It was nearly nine o'clock. But if she was sick, did she have someone...her parents. Jen would call her mom, wouldn't she? They had a close relationship, that much was obvious. Or maybe she'd go to their house? She was fine. She had to be fine.

He eyed his phone and grabbed it before he could stop himself. He opened a text, tapped out a brief message and hit send.

No more. He wasn't going to chase her anymore tonight. He'd see her at the office...and if he didn't, if she was still sick, he'd go by with some flowers and soup. Maybe something that would cheer her up.

"Got time for lunch?" David tucked his hands in his pockets and leaned against the door frame.

Jen looked up, panic in her expression before she schooled her face to be impassive. He saw signs of tears in her blood-shot eyes and swollen nose. "No. Sorry. There's a lot going on today so I'm going to have to take a rain check."

David frowned. She sounded off. He stepped into the office and started to close the door when she held up a hand.

"Please. I really don't have time. I'll give you a call...later."

"Are you okay?"

She looked up and pinned him with her stare. "No. I'm really not. But I will be. Please go."

David hesitated in the doorway as she went back to work, carefully not looking in his direction. He rubbed the back of his neck and turned. What was going on?

Back in his office, he stared at his computer monitor. What happened at lunch yesterday? It had to be something bad. Sara'd had news—but what kind of news would have made Jen give him such a cold shoulder? He barely knew Sara. He grabbed his cell and scrolled through his contacts until he found Ben. He frowned. Maybe he should go down and try to get her to talk to him—or work on her at home after the workday was over? But if she wasn't going to tell him what was going on, didn't he need to have an idea going in? He hit call.

"Ben Taylor."

"Ben, hi, it's David Pak?"

"Hi, David. I thought I might be hearing from you today. I was actually considering calling you."

David closed his eyes and leaned back in his chair. "What's going on?"

"Rebecca said Sara found a profile for you on an online dating site—a recent one. She showed it to Jen and Jen took off like she was going to be ill. Neither of them have heard from her since, though Rebecca spent a lot of last night trying to call."

The bottom of the world fell out from under him. That dating profile. He'd meant to delete it. He'd never really looked for a match—hadn't even finished filling out the questionnaire, though that hadn't stopped the daily emails of potential matches based on his partial survey.

"You there?"

"Yeah, I'm here. I...could explain, but I'm not sure there's a point."

"Try me." There was an undercurrent of hostility in Ben's voice. Was David going to lose his friends, in addition to Jen, because of this?

"Our first date was horrible. You know that—even she admits that. And so, on a whim, I opened an account, though I never even finished the setup process before I realized that Jen was worth another chance. That she was special and I wasn't going to find someone better—or at least that I didn't want to look until I gave her, us, another chance. I talked to Jackson about it."

"As it happens, I already talked to Jackson. He's fully on your side, if that helps. Given what you just said, I'm inclined to be as well. Though that might cause some problems with my wife. Jen and Sara are two of her best friends. They've seen her through some of the darkest parts of her life. She's fiercely protective."

"I understand that. I'm glad Jen has someone like that on her side. I...I can't even get her to talk to me though. How can we get past this—how do I fix it—if she won't talk to me?" David pinched the bridge of his nose. It was like something out of those cheesy movies his sisters watched. He never dreamed it could happen like that in real life. Didn't people just have rational conversations and hash through their problems? That's what his parents always did.

"I don't know, man. But...here's the thing."

David winced. That was never a good intro. "Yeah?"

"Unless Jen tells Rebecca otherwise before then, she doesn't want you at the wedding, and she convinced Paige that you shouldn't be there. I tried to tell her she was being unreasonable. But, like I said, fierce."

There went one plan that had been forming in his mind. He'd been willing to bet she wouldn't cause a scene at a wedding. Maybe it was for the best. "Yeah, okay."

"I hope you can work it out. I'll be praying for you."

David scoffed. That was the only possible thing that was going to fix this. Prayer. "Thanks."

"Hi, Mom, Dad." David called out as he let himself into his parent's house, a bag of ice cream sundae fixings in his hand.

"In the den."

He smiled at the surprise in his mom's voice and made his way to where they sat, watching a movie on TV. "I brought ice cream. Anyone game?"

"Whatcha got?" His dad looked up and squinted at the bag. "Oh yeah, I want some."

"Why are you here, David? I thought you had a wedding that you were going to with Jen?"

David sighed. Of course his mom didn't forget. "We had a disagreement. I guess. I got uninvited."

"What?" His mother started to stand. He smiled in spite of himself. Even now, his mom was his best defender.

"Sit down, Mom, it's okay. They're her friends more than mine." That stung. The truth of it. He'd broken away from his usual group—not that it had been hard to do, it was time, really—but now he had nothing. Sure, he could probably go back to them, but the thought of hanging out as they tried to one-up each other held no interest. He wanted to be with Jen. With Jackson and Paige, Ben and

Rebecca, Zach and Amy. They were real. Genuine. Fun to be around. "I'll go get bowls."

When he got back, his mom already had the ice cream open and the toppings arranged on the coffee table. She ran her hand up and down his arm. "You're okay?"

David swallowed the lump in his throat. "No, Mom. I'm not."

"Oh, baby. What can you do to fix things?"

He flipped the lid off the ice cream and began to scoop. "I don't know. She won't talk to me. I've tried going to her office, but she freezes me out. And when I call or text, she ignores me. I haven't gone by, mostly because I don't want to cause a scene and have her neighbors talking. It's likely I'd end up banging on her door while she ignored me and refused to come out. I don't know what else to try."

"Your—her—friends, do they know what's happened?"

He squirted whipped cream on top of his ice cream and explained the misunderstanding.

"Oh, David. Online dating?" His father shook his head. "Your grandfather and I would have found you someone. How is that any different?"

David winced. Put that way, maybe it wasn't. But...it took the choice out of his hands, didn't it? "It doesn't matter, Dad. I never did anything with it. I'm in love with Jen. More than that, I know in my heart she's the woman God has for me."

His father scoffed and tapped his bowl with his spoon. "That may be true, but you've messed it up."

"Oh, hush. You made some missteps when we were courting. I nearly went to my father to call off our marriage three times."

His father looked away.

"Seriously?" David dug into his ice cream. "You've never mentioned that before."

"I respect your father. I never wanted his children to know he could be a fool."

"We fixed it, didn't we?" His father frowned at his mother. "I apologized."

"True. You did. And I didn't call off the wedding." She smiled and patted his hand. "My point is this, sometimes men are stupid. What you did, David, was stupid."

He hunched his shoulders. She was right. Even if it pained him to admit it.

"You've deleted the account now, right?"

He winced. "I keep forgetting."

His mother tsked. "Go. Use the computer in the kitchen and do it now. You can take your ice cream. Come back when you're finished and we'll figure out what you should do next."

David started to stand then pursed his lips. "I...might have a better idea."

25

Jen pulled out a chair next to Sara. "Where's your date?"

"Getting some punch. I can't believe they didn't rent a restaurant or something. This is so..."

"Lovely? Them? And the food's from Season's Bounty, so it's not like it isn't catered." Jen frowned. Sara had been negative the whole time, complaining that there weren't many people, the side chapel of the church was too plain. Then again, Sara loved the wedding shows on TV where people spent more on one day than she made in a year. Those shows made Jen's stomach turn. Maybe she wanted a little more frills than Paige and Jackson had, but extravagant wasn't on her wish list. To each her own.

"Speaking of dates, where'd Brandon go?"

"Braedon. He got a phone call as we were on the way up. He stepped outside to take it." Jen shrugged. She'd only asked him on the off chance David showed up. She hadn't wanted to be there alone, like she was pining for him. Even if she was. David. His name was like an ice pick through her heart. Had he really been cheating on her?

Sara frowned. "I shouldn't have shown you the dating app, should I?"

"You thought you were doing the right thing." Maybe it was the right thing. She deserved better than someone who'd cheat, didn't she? But was he cheating? She didn't trust herself to ask—after all, what if he said no? She'd have to choose whether or not she believed him. The heaviness that had been her constant companion throughout the week snuggled closer, blurring the edges of her vision. She just had to make it through cake and then she could escape. She'd go home, turn off her phone, and lose herself in the beautiful oblivion of sleep. At least until two a.m. when the barrage of questions and doubt started. But then she had her puzzle. Even if she couldn't make sense of her life, eventually she could find where pieces of the puzzle were supposed to go. Maybe when she finished the whole thing she'd have figured out a way to move on.

"For what it's worth, I'm sorry." Sara brushed her fingers over Jen's hand. "I didn't want you to get hurt."

"I know." Jen forced a smile.

Braedon strode across the room and rested his hand on Jen's shoulder. "Hey. I have to go. That was—"

Jen waved away his explanation. "Don't worry about it. I can find a ride home."

"You're sure?"

She nodded. She could always call a cab if push came to shove. There wasn't any hope of a relationship with the guy. They were co-workers. Well, technically he reported to her, and besides, there wasn't any spark. The few times they'd tried to have a conversation on the ride to the church, they'd ended up reverting back to talking about work. They didn't have any other intersecting points of interest. And frankly, despite only being three years older than him, he was too young.

"Okay. Thanks. I'll see you Monday."

"Sure. Thanks for coming."

He waved before disappearing through the crowd. Jen sighed. Another failure.

"He's not your type."

Jen raised an eyebrow at Sara. "Yeah? Well, who is my type?"

Sara blushed and turned away.

At least Sara understood what she'd done. The first guy in...ever, who was exactly what she was looking for. Jen pushed the chair back and stood. "I'm going to go see if they need help with anything."

Maybe if she kept busy she'd stop looking for David at every table.

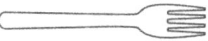

"Is this seat taken?"

Jen looked up, her eyes widening as she saw David. "Yes."

"That's too bad." He sat down in the pew and dragged his laptop bag onto his lap. "I won't stay, if you don't want me to, but I'd like you to see something before I go."

She shook her head. He couldn't be doing this. Not here, in church. She checked her phone. There were still twenty minutes until the service started. That's what she got for being early. If the insomnia would go away, she could get back to sleeping past her alarm, and missing the opening song. And then she wouldn't be trapped next to the last person in the world she wanted to talk to. She crossed her arms. She could get up and barge through the cluster of old people at the other end of the pew. Or jump over the back. But that would cause a scene and be even more humiliating than it already was.

"Here." David angled his laptop so she could see. "This is my account on the dating site. Yes, I have one—well, half of one. If you look here, you'll see the prompt to finish filling out my profile. And, if you look here." He clicked on the account history tab. "You'll see that I never did any searches or sent any messages. So, I have the account. And I made it after our disastrous date, I'll admit to that bad judgment. But I never used it. It's always been you. Even when I wasn't sure why."

She blinked back tears and looked at his laptop before inclining her head. It was an acknowledgement. Nothing more.

"Now, this is me deleting that account." David clicked several times, pausing with each confirmation pop up and waiting until her eyes darted over to look. He closed the laptop, slid it back into its case, and stood. "Like I said, it's always been you. I think it's always going to be you, Jen. And so I hope, and pray, that you'll come back to me. Because I don't want to spend the rest of my life without you in it."

Jen's heart raced. What was she supposed to say to that? No words formed her mind.

He offered a tight smile. "Goodbye."

He walked down the aisle and ran into Ben and Rebecca as he was leaving. They looked confused. David spoke, briefly, but he was too far away to hear.

Rebecca sat next to Jen and let out a breath. "Maybe we were too hard on him. Did you realize he's in love with you?"

Tears spilled down her cheeks. Jen buried her face in her hands. *Oh, God...what am I supposed to do?*

She'd made it through the week. Mostly. She just had to get through today and then the weekend, blissfully free of any obligations, stretched out in front of her. She just had to get out of bed and start the day. Jen continued to stare at the ceiling while her alarm beeped. She should turn that off. She closed her eyes and rolled over. The alarm chimed in tune with her heartbeat. Which at least made it clear she had one. That was a step in the right direction. She sighed and, gathering her energy, rolled back over and flung her arm toward the alarm. The noise stopped. Now to get out of bed.

Tribble whined and jumped up on the bed, her pink tongue darting out to leave a wet, slimy trail on her cheek.

"Ugh. Tribble, down." Jen frowned and pushed herself into a sitting position. Tribble danced around her feet, but even that didn't poke a hole in the gray clouds that surrounded everything she saw. "Come on."

Jen shuffled down the hall and to the patio door. She leaned against the frame while Tribble dashed outside and did her business at the very edge of the grass. It must be a lot later than usual. How long had she laid there? Didn't matter. If she had to work later than usual to make sure she got her hours in, it wasn't the end of the world. Or, honestly, she could leave and skirt on a few hours. It wasn't like everyone else didn't do that occasionally. Just because she had always walked the straight and narrow didn't mean she had to keep doing it. That was another thing that didn't matter.

Did anything matter?

Tribble bounced back to the door and grinned up at her, tongue lolling out the side of her mouth. Jen sighed. "Now you want to eat, right?"

She followed the dog into the kitchen and poured food into her bowl then stood in front of the refrigerator. She should eat something too. Her stomach twisted. Hunger? Nausea? Whatever. She closed the fridge and, with a glance at Tribble who had finished gulping her food and was now lapping up water, trudged back to her bedroom. She'd take a shower, go to work, come home, and the week would be over. Another fifty years of that and life would be over, finally, too.

Shoulders slumped, Jen twisted the knob in the shower to hot, as tears ran down her face.

26

David ducked around the corner as Jen came down the hallway. Though it wasn't like she'd see him. She walked with her head down, shoulders stooped. Almost as if she had a heavy weight pressing down on her from above. She probably wouldn't see him if he stood directly in front of her and blocked the path. She'd just step around him and continue to her office on autopilot. His heart ached—not just because she still wouldn't speak to him, despite what he'd done on Sunday—but for how clearly she was hurting. All week, David had been getting in early and sneaking into her office to leave her a little something that would, hopefully, brighten her day at least a tiny bit. Each morning, it was gratifying to see that she hadn't thrown the previous day's gift away.

They weren't anything amazing—a Bible verse on an index card, a pretty picture he'd printed from the Internet and put in a frame, chocolate—but she had to know they were from him. And maybe it would remind her that he cared about her. She'd lost more weight. Clearly she was one of the people who lost their appetite when they were depressed. Ji had been a comfort eater and had ballooned up several sizes before they'd found a combination of medication and counseling that helped her.

"What is this?"

David grinned and snuck closer. It was too bad he couldn't see her. Today, since it was Friday, he'd gone for something a little flashier. The tulips in a riot of colors at the grocery store had caught his eye this morning. Even as he tried to find something smaller, he'd kept the vision of those flowers. So he'd given in. From the sound of things, he'd made the right choice.

He scooted out the door into the elevator lobby and ducked into the stairwell. He jogged up the stairs to his floor. That would be his exercise for the day. Unless his lunchtime plan failed. In which case, he might need to beat a hasty retreat again.

When the meeting finally ended, David checked the time and groaned. He wasn't going to be able to catch Jen for lunch, most likely. Not that she was probably going to agree to come, but he'd given her space and it was time to ask. And then keep asking until she either agreed or told him to go away. He'd go down and ask anyway. He still needed something and maybe he could talk her into an ice cream cone.

Except that someone was sitting in his guest chair. He sighed and rearranged his plans for the afternoon. Unexpected visitors—especially lately—never ended up being a good thing.

"Hope you weren't waiting long, our meeting ran...Jen?" He stopped his default spiel when he was close enough to recognize her. David closed his office door, set his laptop and folders on his desk, hooked his other guest chair and tugged it around so he was facing her, and sat. "Hi."

Jen pressed her lips together before she spoke. "Hi. And I wasn't waiting long. I...called up to see if you were in. The receptionist let me know when it looked like the meeting was wrapping up."

"Smart. I'm glad you came up." He took a deep breath. It was a difficult balance to avoid pulling her into his arms and spilling every thought and feeling he'd had in the last two weeks. He'd missed her to the point of pain. But her being here didn't automatically mean she was back. Better to take it slow. Casual. "Want to go grab a bite?"

She twisted her fingers in her lap. "Maybe. First, I have a couple of questions."

"Okay."

She took several deep breaths and stared over his shoulder before her gaze cut over to meet his. "Why haven't you given up?"

His eyebrows lifted. "Because I think you're worth fighting for. I apologized once, but I'll do it again. I'm sorry. For opening the dating profile, for how you found out about it, and for getting so distracted, or lazy, that I didn't delete it the handful of times it occurred to me, which could have avoided the problem altogether."

Jen shook her head. "But why? Why, when you see how big a mess I am, would you still want anything to do with me? Even if just as friends?"

He reached out and closed his hand over hers. "I don't want to just be friends. Not if there's a chance we can be more. I love you. And maybe this is the wrong time to say that. I don't want to pressure you. You don't have to feel the same way, yet, though I hope at some point you will. But, when you get down to it, that's the reason."

"You deserve so much better." Jen looked down and tried to pull her hand free.

David tightened his grip. "No. I'm incredibly grateful God saw fit to bring you into my life and give me the chance to deserve you."

A tear slipped down her cheek, followed quickly by another and then more.

He scooted closer so their knees touched and drew her to him, slipping his arms around her. He began to gently rub her back, swallowing the words that wanted to come. Ji said so many times that the people who helped the most were the ones who would let her feel whatever emotions needed to come out, without asking her to calm down. He could do that, even when his heart was breaking for the woman in his arms.

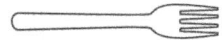

David shifted the take-out bag to his other arm and knocked on Jen's door. He hadn't expected her to agree to his idea of dinner and a movie at her place, not when she'd been so mortified after her crying jag. Maybe this was a crack in the icy shell she'd been building to keep him out. He prayed it was.

"You came. I was expecting a call saying you had other plans, or just didn't want to come." She stepped back and opened the door the rest of the way. "Come on in."

It was the depression talking. David refused to be hurt by her words. She was trying to see if she could push him away, and he wasn't going anywhere. Not until she asked him to and he believed it was really her, not her illness, doing the asking. "I brought Thai. Figured that might a nice change from the usual. And there's one of those rental vending machines in the same shopping center, so I brought a selection to choose from. Oh, and I got Tribble a treat, too."

At the word 'treat', the dog's head lifted and her tail began to wag. David grinned and dug into the bag until he found the extra-large cookie bone. It had required an extra trip, but the pet store wasn't that far out of the way, and Jen's smile was worth it. As was Tribble's.

"Why don't we eat in here? The couch is comfier, and then we can start the movie right away."

He nodded, taking in the faded pajama pants and long sleeve t-shirt she wore. He'd changed after work as well, but into jeans and a light sweater. Should he have tried to convince her to go out? Would being beyond the walls of her apartment help or hinder? Too late now, but something to consider for the future. He set the bag of food down on the coffee table, pushed aside the pile of blankets that were crumpled at one end of the couch, and sat. He pulled out a handful of DVDs in clear plastic cases and offered them to Jen. "Dealer's choice."

Jen plopped on the couch and tucked her feet under her before she started flipping through the movies.

David pulled two containers of Pad Thai from the bag along with plastic forks and a handful of napkins. "I forgot drinks."

"Um. There's water in the kitchen?"

He chuckled as he stood. He'd find the glasses. Couldn't be that hard. He stepped in to the kitchen and took a deep breath. Wow. No wonder she didn't want to eat in here. Dishes were piled in the sink, half a sandwich sat on a plate on the counter, and there was a pot of dried out macaroni and cheese sitting on the stove. He opened the cabinet where he would store cups and was rewarded with mostly bare shelves. With the exception of two mugs. Frowning, he checked the other cupboards. Nope, that was the right one.

Shrugging, he took down the mugs, filled them at the tap, and went back into the living room. "Here we are. I wasn't sure how spicy you liked things, so I went medium and brought some assorted sauces in case you needed to jazz it up. Can't go backward, unfortunately."

"Medium should be fine. You're really going to watch one of these movies?"

David nodded. "What'd you choose?"

After giving him a long look, Jen held out one of the movies, her expression almost defiant. He glanced at the title and covered a chuckle with a cough. What was it about impossible paranormal young adult romances that appealed to depressed women? It had been his sister's recommendation. She promised him that, at the end of the day, there would be enough vampire fights to keep it semi-interesting.

He popped open the cover and took out the disc, checking the back to be sure it wasn't scratched. He eyed her player. The system looked straightforward, which was good. He wasn't exactly a whiz when it came to troubleshooting audio visual equipment, much to the amusement of his family. Computers? Yes. DVD players? Not so much. He slid the disc in, grabbed the remote from beside the TV, and went back to sit next to Jen.

David took her hand and offered a short prayer for the food before hitting play. "Ready?"

She opened the container of food and breathed in the steam before turning to give him a slight smile. "Yeah. Thanks."

He patted her leg before reaching for his own food and leaning back. It was nice. Cozy.

He wanted to get used to it.

27

Tribble was licking her face again. Jen pried open one eye. The couch. Why was she on the couch?

"Okay, okay." She rubbed her eyes and sat up, the blankets sliding down to the floor, nearly burying Tribble, who yipped in protest. Jen squinted at the clock on the DVD player. Ten a.m.? How was that possible? She hadn't slept that long, or well, in weeks. With a jaw-cracking yawn, she shuffled to the patio and unlocked the door for Tribble. This late in the morning, there was liable to be a mess somewhere, but she'd get to that when she found it.

Leaving the door open, she went into the kitchen and stopped, her jaw dropping. The counters gleamed. The sink was empty. The light on her dishwasher indicated a completed cycle, and the few non-dishwasher items were stacked neatly on a towel. He'd done her dishes and cleaned the kitchen.

When had she fallen asleep? She had a vague memory of stretching out with her feet in his lap maybe thirty minutes into the movie, after she'd finished the Pad Thai. The entire container of it. Had she drifted off that quickly? And instead of waking her, or just going home, he'd cleaned the kitchen?

Heat burned across her cheeks and she closed her eyes. Why had she let him come over when so much of her house was a disaster? The bathroom. Had he gone into the bathroom? It didn't bear thinking about. He must think she was a slob of epic proportions. Except...he'd been over before. When things weren't as bad. He had to know it wasn't always that bad. And she couldn't change it now, so...best not to dwell on it.

Tribble danced in and sat by her bowl, turning a pitiful gaze in her direction. "I know. He cleaned up. Did you help him?"

Jen scooped dry food into the bowl, then squatted and ran her hand down Tribble's head and back. How long had it been since she took the time to really interact with the dog? Two weeks. Everything was two weeks. Since she'd found out about David's online dating thing. It had thrown her more than she wanted to admit even to herself.

Their first date had been terrible. No one questioned that. And she'd even considered being done right then. So why did it bother her so much that he'd actually done something—or started to? When he'd showed her on Sunday that it never got past the signing up stage, something in her cracked, just a little. She wanted—needed—to believe that she was worth someone's time. That it was possible for someone to love her.

And he'd shown her that—both before Sara's revelation and since.

Yesterday, in his office, he'd told her he loved her. She hadn't really heard the words through the soupy fog of depression. Now, looking around her kitchen, those same words rang in her head, the truth of them obvious.

He loved her.

And she loved him.

It was time to admit it. Out loud.

"Where's David?" Rebecca turned and surveyed the sanctuary as everyone filed out of the service. "I thought you said you two patched things up?"

"We're...on the way to it, at least. I don't know. I expected him to be here too, to be honest. Maybe he thinks it'd be awkward with you all? Uninviting him from the wedding was kind of a blow." Jen shrugged.

Rebecca sighed. "Maybe so. But what were we supposed to do?"

"I'm not complaining. Just trying to think of why he isn't here. Speaking of people who aren't here, where's Sara?"

"She's been dodging my calls. I don't know what the deal is. Though she's pretty torn up about what she did. She told me she's worried you won't forgive her."

Jen frowned. "I thought we cleared that up."

"She doesn't think so. She says you haven't answered any of her calls."

"I haven't answered anyone's calls. Did you tell her that?" Jen rubbed the back of her neck. What a mess. "I'll give her a call this afternoon."

"Are you coming to lunch?"

Jen shook her head. "Not today."

"You okay?" Rebecca's face was a cloud of concern. "You've been off—don't you think you should just snap out of it? I mean, you and David have figured things out, so...cheer up."

Jen forced a smile. Why hadn't she thought of that? Just get over it and move on. Did no one understand? David did. What a blessing he was. "Right. I'll work on that."

"So what are you going to do if you're not coming to lunch?"

"I have some cleaning I need to do—I've gotten a little behind."

Rebecca nodded. "All right. Lunch this week sometime?"

"Sure. Text me." Jen gathered her Bible and purse and headed toward the door. She'd go home and clean, though she'd made good headway on that yesterday after being inspired by her sparkling kitchen. But she had a stop to make first.

Butterflies danced in her stomach as she rode the elevator to David's floor. Would he even be home? If he'd gone back to his old church, did he go to his parents for lunch? Or his sister's? Hadn't he said they usually spent at least part of Sunday together? She took a deep breath and pressed a hand to her belly. No way to find out without knocking.

She waited then knocked again.

After a minute, locks clicked and a rumpled David answered the door, confusion written on his face. "Hey, Jen."

"Hi. I...maybe I should go. I thought..."

"Don't go. I'm just groggy. Late night. Come in?" David stepped aside.

She lifted the takeout bag. "I brought lunch. I—we—I missed you at church. I wanted to say thank you for Friday. You didn't have to clean the kitchen. I'm sorry it was such a mess."

"Hey, don't worry about it. I've seen dirty dishes before." He smiled, his eyes lighting with humor. "Come sit down, what'd you bring?"

"Nothing fancy. I picked up some Peruvian chicken and yucca fries." Jen pulled a chair out at the table and sat. "Can I ask why you didn't come to church?"

"Of course. Couple of reasons. First, I had a late night last night. I got an email in the morning with a proposal, due by midnight, that they needed one final check on. Of course it wasn't quite finished, so it was a mad rush with lots of back and forth. I ended up not making any friends, but the bid is better because of it." David peered into the bag and pulled out the two containers. "Beyond that, though...I wasn't sure if everyone would be okay with me being there. From what Ben said before the wedding, I think I'm kind of persona non grata right now."

Jen reached out and tentatively laid her hand on his. "They're just protective. I'm sorry. It's my fault."

"No. It's mine. I never should have—"

She touched his lips with her finger. "It's done. Behind us. I'd rather focus on the fact that you not only were willing to watch that ridiculous movie with me, but you let me sleep and cleaned my kitchen."

"And played with Tribble. Honestly, I'm kind of surprised her yapping didn't wake you, but you were out cold."

Jen chuckled. Poor baby. She needed to make sure she spent more time with her puppy when she got home. It wasn't Tribble's fault that Jen had sunk so far under her ability to cope. "Thanks. She, and I, appreciate it."

"Any time."

28

David gathered his laptop and checked his cell. Jen was supposed to text him and let him know if she wanted to try the young professionals Wednesday Bible study with him. Nothing. He tapped out a quick text. Maybe she'd still be up for it.

As he hit the elevator call button, his phone buzzed. Seeing Jen's picture made him smile. "Hey. You in?"

"I can't. I need to go check on Sara. She hasn't been at work since Monday and even then, Rebecca said she was off. I don't know what's going on, but I need to make sure she's okay. I'm worried about her. This breakup is hitting her harder than usual."

"Want me to come along?" Hopefully she'd say no. Offering was the right thing to do, but he didn't know Sara all that well. And he was a guy.

"I really do. But I don't think it's the right thing. Thank you for offering though. Can you pray? I'm scared of what I'm going to find."

David waved off the elevator when it opened and the people inside looked at him expectantly. "What do you mean? Do you think she's suicidal?"

"I don't know what to think. This is just so unlike her. And...I know what it's like to believe there's no way through something. That the only good answer is to give up the fight."

He closed his eyes. "I'm so sorry, sweetheart."

"It's been a while since it's been that bad. But it doesn't change the knowing. That ledge is horrible and comforting all at once and you're torn between the agony of living and the terror of leaping.

None of the options are good, and you just want to find the one that makes the pain stop soonest. I don't know if she's there—but if she is, I have to at least try to help her see that no matter how dark it is on the cliff, if you look around, and sometimes you have to look pretty hard, I won't lie, but if you really look, there's always at least a tiny reason to stay. But if you give up on that handful of hope, no matter how meager it is, the only one who loses is you."

David's eyes filled. He didn't understand, really, having never walked through that soul-deep level of darkness. Even walking beside someone as they battled their way through wasn't the same. But the little sliver of knowledge he had from watching his sister, and seeing Jen's own struggles for the short time they'd known one another, left him in awe of her strength. "You're amazing. I'll be praying."

"I'm really not. I don't have it figured out. Some days the only hope I'm holding onto is the promise that Jesus won't forsake me, despite it feeling like He already has. I'll call you later."

He hit end and leaned against the wall, eyes closed. *Jesus, be with Jen. Give her Your words and Your strength. And be near to Sara.* With a deep breath, he pushed off the wall and hit the elevator button again. He'd go and give the study a try. And if he couldn't focus on that, he could always find a quiet place to pray.

"I wasn't sure you'd be in today after you were with Sara so late last night."

Jen looked up with a wan smile. "And yet you brought two coffees?"

David laughed. "Well, maybe they're both for me?"

"Not buying it. Gimme." She reached for one of the cups.

Sipping from his own cup, David sat and studied her. Other than looking tired, she seemed okay. "How are you?"

"I'm okay. It was harder than I thought it'd be to talk to her about depression. You get so used to trying to hide it, because people just tell you to cheer up or get over it and you start to believe that your inability to do that is a personal failing. Because most people can just cheer up and decide to move on. The judgment you feel from people who don't get it is...crushing. Sara never understood before, when I'd try to talk to her and Rebecca. I think, now, she has a glimmer of an idea. And while she's not suicidal, thank God, she's going to call the therapist I recommended."

"Good. So she's okay?"

"Not yet. But I think she will be. I also suggested she talk to the pastor. I think some of her trouble is based on what's she's choosing to believe, spiritually. Working through that, finding a way to be consistent in how she views the Bible and how she lives her life, is only going to help."

"Wow."

"I'm not convinced she'll take me up on that one. She still thinks I'm being judgmental and naive. And I'm not trying to say depression is purely a spiritual deficiency, but if you leave it untreated, it can cause one. So I suggested both. And..." Jen sighed, her gaze dropping to her hands. "I probably need to get back into counseling, too. The medication is helping, lots, but maybe not as much as I'd like."

David nodded. "You know that's not failure, right? Needing help?"

She jerked her head up, eyes wide before they filled with tears. "No. I mean, sure, I know it in my head, but my heart? It feels like failure on an epic level. Am I so broken, so useless, that I need medication and a therapist? Aren't we supposed to be able to do this without so much external help?"

"No. I really don't think we are. God designed us to need community. That's why He gave us family, and why we have an inherent craving for friends. At a minimum, we need Him. Getting help doesn't mean you're broken and useless, it means you're strong enough to understand you can't do it on your own. How many people are willing to admit that?" David shook his head. There weren't many.

Jen let out a breath. "You're not just saying that?"

"No. I'm not. I'm proud of you."

She smiled.

David opened his mouth to speak and his phone chimed. "And with that, I need to run before I'm late for a meeting. Are you free Saturday? During the day?"

"Think so, why?"

The idea was just forming, so David smiled. "I'll pick you up around one. Does Tribble do okay in the car?"

Jen looked startled. "Usually. Why?"

"Bring her leash, she can come too."

29

"You're sure they aren't going to mind if I come?" David brushed his hand down the side of his pant leg.

Was he nervous? It was kind of cute. Jen smiled and kissed his cheek before she took his hand in hers. "I promise it's fine. They were upset because I was hurting. That's what friends do. Trust me, okay?"

He nodded and pulled open the door to Season's Bounty. "All right."

Jen squeezed his hand. She never should have said anything to Rebecca about not wanting him at the wedding. Who knew Rebecca would run off to Paige and get her to agree to ask him not to come? Okay, maybe she'd hoped that's what would happen. But it hadn't seemed likely. And it was all water under the bridge now, so there was no point in worrying about it. If people couldn't deal with the fact that they'd worked through their differences, well, too bad.

"Hey!" Rebecca jumped up from a table near the front of the restaurant as they came in. "We're out in front today. Paige said being away for a week left the kitchen staff in need of some serious revamping. So, for now, she set up a big table just for us. I think she's still planning on us being her guinea pigs, but they left menus in case we'd rather go that route. David. It's good to see you. I'm sorry about the whole—"

"Don't worry about it." He smiled and pulled a chair out for Jen, then sat next to her.

Jen reached for his hand. "Who else is coming?"

"I think everyone. Ben's parking the car. Sara said she'd be here and Jackson is in the kitchen working on the first round of food. I think he'll end up being our runner tonight. Gives him a chance to keep tabs on his wife."

Jen laughed. "It's like that, is it?"

"What's like what?" Jackson slid a tray laden with three platters of hors d'oeuvres onto the table. "Sorry about that. I haven't waited tables in...ever. I never waited tables."

"You know, I never did either." Jen shrugged. "You're doing fine."

Rebecca snickered. "I did. Maybe I ought to be running food out for us?"

"Then I wouldn't get to sneak kisses in the kitchen." Jackson grinned and sat. Waving to Ben as he pushed through the main restaurant door.

"I don't understand why the parking garage across the street is so much fuller than it usually is on a Friday night. I finally ended up parking down the street, and only then because I saw someone leaving." Ben kissed Rebecca as he pulled out his chair and sat. "Hey, David. Glad you could make it."

Jen nudged David with her elbow and leaned to whisper in his ear. "Told you."

"Yeah, yeah." He nodded to Ben. "Thanks."

"Sorry I'm late. Parking is...hi, David. I'm so sorry. I didn't think it through and I just—"

David stood and pulled Sara into a hug. "Don't worry about it. Okay? I'd been meaning to delete the thing basically since I opened it, and it's my own fault that I kept getting distracted. How are *you*?"

Sara frowned at Jen.

Jen shrugged. Was she not supposed to have told David? Sara knew how Jen felt about David, so why would she assume Jen wouldn't say anything? She'd never been good at secrets. Sara knew that. Of course, if Sara had said something, Jen would've tried.

"I'm okay. I had a chance to meet the guy Jen recommended today. I think it's going to help. And I may talk to the pastor, too. We'll see."

David nodded. "Good."

Ben, Rebecca, and Jackson exchanged confused looks and Jen chewed her lip. Telling David was one thing, but if the whole group was going to find out, that was going to be up to Sara.

"What's going on?" Rebecca reached for Sara and squeezed her hand as she moved to an empty chair.

Sara sighed. "I guess Jen didn't tell everyone? I'm having a little trouble coping. Luc—well, it's not all Luc. He just pushed me over the edge. Jen helped me understand that there's no harm—no shame—in getting help. So I'm talking to a counselor."

Rebecca nodded. "If you end up not liking him, let me know. I'll give you the name of my therapist."

"You have a therapist?" Jen stared across the table.

Rebecca hunched her shoulders. "Yeah. I've been going for years. I've just never told anyone. It's not something I like to talk about—it's such a ridiculous weakness to not be able to—"

"No. What is this?" David shook his head, a frown etched into his features. "What is wrong with us as a society? As a church? Why do we treat depression as some kind of stigma? It's a disease like any other. You don't just pray your way out of it, you need help. Sorry...hot button."

Jackson chuckled. "I see that. But you're not wrong. I'm glad you're talking to someone, Sara. And that you're willing to share with us. I'll pray for you."

Jen reached for one of the plates in the center of the table. "Now that that's out of the way, are we going to eat?"

"Before we do that, we have news." Rebecca reached for Ben's hand. "It's why we were hoping everyone could come tonight."

Zach and Amy pushed through the restaurant door and waved. "Sorry we're late. What'd we miss?"

"Nothing yet, really." Sara jerked her chin toward Rebecca. "But she was just saying they had news."

"Ah. We do, too." Zach held a chair out for Amy. "But you go first."

Ben and Rebecca exchanged a look before Rebecca spoke. "I'm pregnant."

Jen laughed and joined in the scattered clapping that worked around the table. "Congratulations, guys."

"Yeah, man. That's great." Jackson slapped Ben on the back.

"You're not upset, are you?" Sara shifted in her chair and looked at Rebecca.

"Not at all. We're not kids. And while sure, we might have wanted to wait a year or two, this is a good thing. God's plans are better than ours." Ben rubbed Rebecca's shoulder and looked at Zach. "What's up with you two?"

Zach cleared his throat. "We got married this afternoon. That's why we're late. The courthouse was busier than we anticipated."

Jen stared up at the ceiling, absently stroking Tribble's head. What a pleasant night. Good food. Good conversation. And maybe, between Rebecca, Sara, and herself, they'd managed to raise awareness within their little circle.

David had been amazing. His struggles with his sister's depression had given him such insight. And compassion. He'd shared, a little, about her struggles. And for the first time in a long time, Jen had been willing to talk about her own. And then to find out that she wasn't alone in feeling inadequate.

Was it simply part of the human condition to struggle like that?

In some ways, that was a comfort. She wasn't alone. Even her friends who always seemed to have everything together struggled at some level with those same thoughts and feelings. Maybe not to the same degree, but they understood. Not the full extent, but enough that it was clear she wasn't alone.

That left her lighter inside than she'd been in a long time.

She chuckled and rolled to her side, burrowing under the covers. Rebecca and Ben were expecting. They'd be great parents. And it'd be fun to have a baby to spoil. She'd always loved babysitting. It was unlikely they'd refuse her offer to help out—who didn't love a night out every now and then? Still, it was a big change. December wedding and not three months later, a baby. But if anyone could do it, it'd be them.

The big surprise was Zach and Amy. They were still having a big Christmas wedding, it would just be their public vows and a chance for everyone to dress up and celebrate their commitment. They weren't, at this point, planning on telling many people that they were already married. Amy's parents had gone to the courthouse, and they'd let Zach's family know. But beyond that they were planning to keep it quiet.

Jen scoffed. She gave them a week before they let the cat out of the bag.

Jen took the leash down from the hook where she stored it and clipped it to Tribble's collar. "You ready, girl? David's taking us on an adventure. I don't know where, but it's a lovely day. And we get to be with David, so that's a bonus, right?"

Tribble danced around her feet, tangling her legs in the leash.

Jen laughed and let go of the end. She stepped out of the coil and reached for her dog's collar. "Sit. Sit, girl."

Quivering, Tribble almost sat, her tail end hovering over the ground, not quite touching.

"Good girl." Jen grabbed the leash and looped it over her hand as someone knocked. "That's got to be him, let's go."

She tucked her phone in her pocket and hooked her purse over her shoulder before opening the door.

David looked amazing. Dark jeans and a collared shirt were casual, but on him they weren't sloppy. Should she have worn something nicer? Her jeans were older, faded and comfortable, but with the dog in tow, she hadn't wanted something too nice. She'd said Tribble did okay in the car, but the truth was, sometimes she did and sometimes she didn't.

"You set?"

She nodded. "We are. No hints on what we're doing?"

He grinned and shook his head. "Nope. Come on. You'll figure it out soon enough."

David backed out of the parking spot and before long they were on the Beltway, headed toward I-66.

"So we're headed into the city? I wonder if the cherry blossoms are still on the trees?"

"Told you you'd figure it out. They should be. The festival was last weekend, but everything I've read says they're still lovely. I thought we could walk along the tidal basin. My mom used to drag the whole family down every year for photos with the cherry blossoms. Even when she stopped, I've been making my way downtown every spring, whenever I can, to enjoy them. I probably wouldn't admit it to her, but I miss those family photo shoots."

Jen laughed. "My mom tried it one year. We ended up with so many tourists in our photos she never did it again. I think it was the weekend of the festival though. So that definitely didn't help us."

"I imagine not. Usually, if you can go the weekend before or after, you still get the blossoms, but without quite as many tourists." He shifted lanes as they crossed the bridge over the Potomac. "The big question is whether or not we'll find parking. I'm hoping we can, but we may end up needing to find a lot, pay, and then walk. That okay?"

"Of course. If Tribble gets tired, I'll just carry her. That's the nice thing about a tiny dog."

"Sure. Though the big dogs don't get tired as fast. So...tradeoff."

He had a point. Though big dogs weren't really her favorite. As much as she loved dogs, the big ones...they still made her palms sweat.

They wound through the streets surrounding the National Mall. Jen scoured the parking areas for empty spaces or cars with their brake lights on, anything that might indicate they were getting ready to pull out. "Oh—over there, right."

David followed her pointing finger and nodded. "Got it. Let's see if we can beat everyone else."

Flicking on his turn signal, David zipped across two lanes of traffic and eased into the parking spot. "Good eye. Looks like we have two hours?"

Jen craned her neck to see the sign and nodded. "Sounds right."

David tapped his phone. "I set an alarm to be sure. I don't think it's going to be a problem, but I'd just as soon not end up with a parking ticket."

Tribble sniffed the grass at the curb and squatted while Jen waited for David to come around to the sidewalk. He took her hand and squeezed. "Let's go this way—we'll get to see more of the trees, and the water."

As they walked, Jen looked around. There were plenty of people out doing exactly as they were, but it wasn't so crowded that you were squeezed on the sidewalk. The delicate pink, almost white, blossoms of the cherry trees were the perfect crown to the horizon, a stark contrast to the blue water. "I'd forgotten how beautiful this is. I don't come downtown as much as I should. We're here by all this history, and yet I get so caught up in living that I forget what's right in my back yard."

David nodded. "I come downtown for work sometimes, or for volunteer activities with some of the politicians I try to help out.

But I haven't been to a museum in...ages. You want to do that sometime?"

"Yeah, that'd be great."

"Oh. Let's stop here." David pulled her into a little copse of trees where a stone lantern sat. "Look through the middle."

Jen leaned over and peered through the hole in the lantern, the stone creating a frame for the blooms on the other side of the Tidal Basin. "I love that."

Tribble wrapped the leash around her legs and then David's, dragging them closer together.

Jen laughed and started to reach for the dog's collar when David slipped his arm around her waist.

"I love you, Jen. I said it the other day, and I know the timing was off. But it's just as true today, maybe more true. Truer?" David frowned and rested his forehead on hers. "I want you to know that. I'm in this with you for the long haul."

Heart racing, Jen wrapped her arms around him, ignoring Tribble's excited yipping and the leash tightening around her legs. "I heard you. I'll admit, I wasn't sure what to think. I thought maybe you were confusing love with pity, or something else. But I don't think that anymore. I'm so grateful you're in my life. I love you, too."

A smile played at the corners of his mouth as he lowered his lips to hers.

Want a free book?

If you enjoyed *A Handful of Hope* and would like to read another book of mine, you can receive a free download of *Courage to Change (Grant Us Grace Book 2)*, simply by signing up for my newsletter here: http://bit.ly/1NsVtAo The first book in the Grant Us Grace series is free on all e-book platforms.

Author's Note

Thank you for reading *A Handful of Hope!* I hope that you enjoyed getting to know Jen and David. I would appreciate it if you'd help others enjoy it too by leaving a review on Amazon and Goodreads and telling your friends about it. Any success my books have is owed to readers like you who take the time to tell others about my stories. Thank you, from the bottom of my heart.

In this book, the heroine, Jen, suffers from depression. This is something with which I am, sadly, all too familiar. It's also something that most of us have either experienced or know someone who has. And yet, so often, the church shies away from talking about it in a helpful, meaningful way. It's my prayer that we, as the body of Christ, can find a way to better bind up the wounds of those among us who suffer.

I continue to owe a huge debt of gratitude to my husband and sons for giving me the time to write, my sister for her unflinching support and encouragement, and my critique partners Heather Gray and Jan Elder for catching all the times I use the same word six times in two paragraphs.

More than anything, I'm grateful that God continues to give me words and makes it possible for me to write them down.

I'd love to hear from you! You can connect with me on Facebook my webpage or via email. To stay current with news and occasional giveaways, please subscribe to my newsletter.

About the Author

Elizabeth Maddrey began writing stories as soon as she could form the letters properly and has never looked back. Though her practical nature and love of computers, math, and organization steered her into computer science at Wheaton College, she always had one or more stories in progress to occupy her free time. This continued through a Master's program in Software Engineering, several years in the computer industry, teaching programming at the college level, and a Ph.D. in Computer Technology in Education. When she isn't writing, Elizabeth is a voracious consumer of books and has mastered the art of reading while undertaking just about any other activity.

Elizabeth is the author of more than ten books, both fiction and non-fiction. She lives in the suburbs of Washington, D.C. with her husband and their two incredibly active little boys.

More Books by Elizabeth Maddrey

Contemporary Romance:

"A Splash of Substance" (Taste of Romance Book 1) by Elizabeth Maddrey

She doesn't vote. He works for a Senator. Is it a recipe for romance or disaster?

Paige Jackson has always stayed out of politics, leaving it to God to govern the world. She has enough on her plate as the owner of a catering company founded on convictions to buy local, sustainable fare. Jackson Trent works on Capitol Hill for Senator Carson, putting his beliefs in action to help shape national policy.

Hoping to find high-end clients to keep her business afloat, Paige bids on a contract to cater the Senator's next fundraiser. Shake-ups in the Senator's staff leave Jackson grudgingly in charge of the event. After Paige is chosen as caterer, she and Jackson must work together despite opposing beliefs on how God calls Christians to participate in government. As Paige introduces Jackson to sustainable fare, it's not just the food that piques his interest.

When Senator Carson becomes front-page news in Washington, Paige is sucked into the whirlwind of scandal. Can Jackson convince Paige he wasn't complicit and win her back or has politics burned his chance at love?

"A Pinch of Promise" (Taste of Romance Book 2) by Elizabeth Maddrey

He never forgot his first love.

In the ten years since Ben Taylor last saw Marie, no other woman has measured up. After he meets Rebecca Fisher, the physical therapist rehabilitating his knee, Ben is convinced that she is the same woman he fell in love with so many years ago. She denies it at first, but his persistence causes her to admit the truth. Right before she pushes him away.

To escape a painful negative image created by her father, Rebecca Fischer has constructed an identity completely separate from her past. Seeing Ben, her long lost love, threatens to shatter her intricate illusions. As Ben digs to uncover the truth of who she is, Rebecca must decide if she will trust any man with her wounded heart.

But even if Ben can convince her to admit the truth, how will he be able to trust her love?

"A Dash of Daring" (Taste of Romance Book 3) by Elizabeth Maddrey

God doesn't always call us to do what's easy.

Amy Harris is the after-school care coordinator and long-term sub at the same inner city high school she graduated from. She's always avoided the complications of dating outside her multi-ethnic heritage. Until Zach got hired.

Zach Wilson took a teaching job in a D.C. public school as part of a student-loan forgiveness program. Nearing the end of his commitment, a possibility arises to move to a magnet school in the suburbs. But will leaving the city end things with Amy before they really have a chance to start?

As Zach and Amy work together on the school's annual holiday program, they must each decide if they'll dare to follow where God calls.

Operation Mistletoe (Operation Romance Book 1)

Victoria Spencer hates Christmas.

For the last ten years, disaster has struck on Christmas Eve, leaving Tori dreading the holidays. When she's assigned to cover the light displays for her newspaper, she's determined to spend as little time on the article as possible. Especially once she realizes she's to feature frat boy Gabe "The Babe" Robertson, her former college crush.

Gabe Robertson is a different man than he was in college. Every December, he transforms his acreage into a winter wonderland designed to celebrate the birth of Christ and share God's love with the community. He also uses the lights to raise money for Operation Mistletoe, an organization that sends Christmas to troops stationed overseas.

Unable to set aside her prejudice, Tori looks for ulterior motives in Gabe's actions and determines to dig deeper. Will her investigations destroy any chance of a Merry Christmas?

Operation Valentine (Operation Romance Book 2)

Once love is lost, can it be found?

When Annabelle Elliot returned his engagement ring six years ago, Rick Wentworth buried his broken heart in his job at Intelligence Associates, Inc. Returning from his overseas assignment, a newly awarded contract forces him into daily contact with her.

Working with Rick is a constant reminder of what Annabelle gave up when she let herself be persuaded to focus on a career instead of love. Now, she admits she made a mistake, but reconciliation seems impossible.

Can Annabelle find the courage to let Rick see her heart? And if she does, will he forgive her?

This sweet contemporary Christian romance novella, inspired by Jane Austen's Persuasion, is a modern reminder that love is worth waiting for.

"Kinsale Kisses"

She wants stability. He wants spontaneity. What they need is each other.

Colin O'Bryan cashed out of the software company he founded and started a new life in Ireland. Content to wander from town to town as a traveling musician, he had no goals beyond healing from the betrayals that led to his career change, and finding his next gig.

After the death of her parents, Rachel Sullivan hoped her aunt's B&B on the Southern coast of Ireland would be a place for her to settle and start a new life. Though she can't deny the sparks in Colin's touch, his lack of concern for hearth and home leave her torn.

Can this free-spirited minstrel win her heart or will Rachel choose roots and stability over love?

 "Joint Venture" – (Grant Us Grace Book 0) by Elizabeth Maddrey

Laura Willis is busy planning her wedding to Ryan when she catches him cheating. Again. This time with her best friend. She throws her fist, and her ring, in his face and immerses herself in work at Brenda's House of Hair. But the salon is awash in drama too as Brenda cuts corners and goes on a rampage.

Laura's coworker hairstylist, Matt Stephenson, is searching for other employment options and a new place to live. Deciding to take a risk, he determines to open his own salon and invites Laura to partner with him. Can their friendship survive the undertaking or will this joint venture be more than either of them bargained for?

 "Wisdom to Know" ('Grant Us Grace' series Book 1) by Elizabeth Maddrey

Is there sin that love can't cover?

Lydia Brown has taken just about every wrong turn she could find. When an abortion leaves her overwhelmed by guilt, she turns to drugs to escape her pain. After a single car accident lands her in the hospital facing DUI charges, Lydia is forced to reevaluate her choices.

Kevin McGregor has been biding his time since high school when he heard God tell him that Lydia Brown was the woman he would marry. In the aftermath of Lydia's accident, Kevin must come to grips with the truth about her secret life.

While Kevin works to convince himself and God that loving Lydia is a mistake, Lydia struggles to accept the feelings she has for Kevin, though she fears her sin may be too much for anyone to forgive.

 "Courage to Change" ('Grant Us Grace' series Book 2) by Elizabeth Maddrey

Should you be willing to change for love?

When Phil Reid became a Christian and stopped drinking, his hard-partying wife, Brandi, divorced him. Reeling and betrayed, he becomes convinced Christians should never remarry, and resolves to guard his heart.

Allison Vasak has everything in her life under control, except for one thing. Her heart is irresistibly drawn to fellow attorney and coworker, Phil. Though she knows his history and believes that women should not initiate relationships, she longs to make her feelings known.

As Phil and Allison work closely together to help a pregnant teen, both must re-evaluate their convictions. But when Brandi discovers Phil's new relationship, she decides that though she doesn't want him, no one else can have him either. Can Phil and Allison's love weather the chaos Brandi brings into their lives?

"Serenity to Accept" ('Grant Us Grace' series Book 3) by Elizabeth Maddrey

Is there an exception to every rule? Karin Reid has never had much use for God. There's been too much pain in her life for her to accept that God is anything other than, at best, disinterested or, at worst, sadistic. Until she meets Jason Garcia. After his own mistakes of the past, Jason is committed to dating only Christians. He decides to bend his rule for Karin, as long as she comes to church with him. As their friendship grows, both will have to decide if they'll accept the path God has for them, even if it means losing each other.

Women's Fiction

"Faith Departed" ('Remnants' series Book 1) by Elizabeth Maddrey

Starting a family was supposed to be easy.

Twin sisters June and July have never encountered an obstacle they couldn't overcome. Married just after graduating college, the girls and their husbands remained a close-knit group. Now settled and successful, the next logical step is children. But as the couples struggle to conceive, each must reconcile the goodness of God with their present suffering. Will their faith be strong enough to triumph in the midst of trial?

"Hope Deferred" ('Remnants' series Book 2) by Elizabeth Maddrey

Can pursuit of a blessing become a curse?

June and July and their husbands have spent the last year trying to start a family and now they're desperate for answers. As one couple works with specialists to see how medicine can help them conceive, the other must fight to save their marriage. Will their deferred hope leave them heart sick, or start them on the path to the fulfillment of their dreams?

"Love Defined" ('Remnants' series Book 3) by Elizabeth Maddrey

Dreams Change. Plans Fail.

July and Gareth have reached the end of their infertility treatment options. With conflicting feelings on adoption, they struggle to discover common ground in their marriage. Meanwhile, July's twin sister, June, and her husband, Toby, are navigating the uncertainties of adoption and the challenges of new parenthood. How much stretching can their relationships endure before they snap?

www.ingramcontent.com/pod-product-compliance
Lightning Source LLC
Chambersburg PA
CBHW071303250626

47159CB00004B/1296